Mucky Ducks

Michael E. Meehan

Published by

MELROSE BOOKS

An Imprint of Melrose Press Limited
St Thomas Place, Ely
Cambridgeshire
CB7 4GG, UK
www.melrosebooks.co.uk

FIRST EDITION

Copyright © Michael E. Meehan 2015

The Author asserts his moral right to
be identified as the author of this work

Cover by Melrose Books

ISBN 978-1-910792-08-7
EPUB 978-1-910792-48-3
MOBI 978-1-910792-49-0

Printed and bound in Great Britain by:
CMP (UK) Ltd, G3 The Fulcrum, Vantage Way
Poole, Dorset, BH12 4NU

Index

Introduction	A Tangled Maze	v
Chapter 1	Love Is?	1
Chapter 2	In a State?	14
Chapter 3	Route Map	22
Chapter 4	The Greatest	31
Chapter 5	Four into One	39
Chapter 6	Six Times Two	46
Chapter 7	Loves Hope	56
Chapter 8	Steak and Ale	65
Chapter 9	To the Bar and Back	75
Chapter 10	Walk with ME	84
Chapter 11	Pick and Mix!	95
Chapter 12	I Don't Understand? - It's NOT IDEAL	109
Chapter 13	Love over Law	122
Chapter 14	A Loving Father	127
Chapter 15	Grace and Love	137
Chapter 16	The Journey Begins	144
	Epilogue	153

Introduction

A Tangled Maze

David's head snapped upwards in response to Jay's words. His hand jerked in reflex, sending his glass flying and spilling his drink. David's eyes were wide open like saucers, yet filled with hurt, anger, amazement and the unspoken accusation of 'how dare you…'.

Welcome to the garden of the Black Swan, where the hypocrisy of our adulterous shallow love is tasted and rejected and the fullness of grace is drunk.

Adultery comes in many forms, each weaving a web of deceit as intricate as any Celtic pattern. In the garden, the many knots in our lives are unravelled and lives given new direction, new focus.

George and David, complaisant colleagues, stroll along the river to the Black Swan. They are met along the way by Pete and Jay. The ensuing discussions and presence of Pete and Jay challenges the life attitudes of the two friends. Their adulterous, shallow, temporal love ruled by the five 'P's is challenged, shown for what it is and changed to become one of depth and sincerity. Jay and Pete admonish with forbearance and, in greater measure, encourage with gentleness. They speak about their own lives, demonstrating that they too were considered, in their time, to be 'Mucky Ducks' as much as George and David. Hearts and minds embrace a different way when love filled with grace is accepted – lives are changed.

As you read, whether you are a George or a David, try to move beyond the words into a realm that encourages all, by grace, to live together in friendship, understanding and forgiveness.

Chapter 1

Love Is?

"Goodbye," said George as Barbara, his wife, left for a weekend reunion with old school friends. She eased the car out of the driveway on to the road, George calling after her.

"Safe journey... Have a wonderful time... Happy landings..."

Barbara blew a kiss of acknowledgement and waved farewell as the car headed up the road. The day was bright and sunny so George set about mowing the lawn, with ideas of doing a steady day's work in the garden with possibly the odd rest for a drink or two. The lawn was nearing completion when David, a friend and a worrier type, stuck his head over the fence and asked if he fancied lunch at the Duck.

"My shout, of course," he affirmed.

George's relaxing working day seemingly just took a turn for the better and, not wishing to look a gift horse in the mouth, nodded his acceptance.

"OK, but give me time to finish mowing the lawn and put my tools away."

David wandered off down to the local post office while George finished off and changed ready to go.

"You OK to walk David as Barbara's got the car?" asked George.

"That's fine," he said. "It's a glorious day. We could walk along the river and then up past the old mill race."

Setting off at a gentle amble, the two friends reached the first stile, which led to the river pathway. George, a tall creature with more leg than body, ignored the top two steps of the stile, taking only the first and swinging his legs over it in a fluid, if gangly, motion. David was not so fortunate and was 'vertically challenged'. He had to use both steps up and down, but he had done it all his life so it was no big deal to Him.

As they ambled along chatting amiably, David asked how Barbara was and where she had gone, among a thousand other questions and thoughts.

"She's gone off to a school reunion," said George. "At the old convent place she used to go to school."

"Was she at that school for all her time?" questioned David.

"Pretty much. Right up to going into college anyway," George continued. "We met during our second year at college."

David fell silent, lost in thought trying to work out in his mind how to say what he wanted to say without hurting George. As they walked, the damp grass gave off its fragrance as it was crushed beneath their feet. Hoverflies and other insects danced over the flower heads, landing on one head and then another to feast on the pollen and nectar. George smiled at David, who responded one of those weak, 'I'm in pain' sort of smiles.

"We are good mates David, what's worrying you? Can you not spit it out?"

"I don't know," replied David in a mournful, whiny sort of voice. "It's personal."

Walking a little way further, they came to the kissing gate into the farm field. A small herd of Friesian cattle were lazily eating the lush grass in the field. Some of the cattle looked up at David and George as they opened the gate, then carried on feeding as if to say 'it's only two walkers, no problem'. George went through the wiggle around the gate first and quite deliberately held it to himself, closing it so David could not get through. David looked at George and frowned.

"If we are going to enjoy this walk and a pint at the pub, for both our sakes you need to spit the fur ball out that's stuck in your throat," retorted George.

"I am sorry George. I have so many things on my mind that just seem to overwhelm and drive me down. I don't know what to do or how to sort things out."

George let David through the kissing gate and, as he stepped into the field, gave him a big hug and smiled at him one of those smiles that reaches all parts of the face, including his eyes that seemed to sparkle like crystals turning in a chandelier.

George held David, saying, "It's OK, we are the best of mates aren't we? Talking to me is better than kicking your chin around the floor and I'll do my best not to get upset, cross or laugh at what you say."

David just stood there in George's arms like a dummy, wooden and unmoving. He came back to life with a start as though stung by a wasp, jerking backwards. A tiny pearl of a tear forced its way out from the corner of his eye and he said, "Do you really mean that?"

George just smiled and replied, "Yep."

The quiet resumed as David gathered his scattered thoughts, trying to put them in an order that would allow him to speak.

"George, are you happy with your marriage to Barbara?"

George's eyes popped open like saucers, but only for the wing beat of a bee before a gentle, all-knowing, smile radiated from his face.

"Barbara and I have our ups and downs, but yes I am happy." Both men fell silent for a few strides.

David turned his head to look at George.

"I know you go to church and are a Christian and all that,

but do you never have any doubts about your marriage? Are you always happy and content?"

George drew in a big breath as he thought about what had just been said.

"That's a big bag of questions in such a small sentence my little friend," he said, as he placed his arm around his shoulders and grinned broadly.

"First off, can I just make a very broad statement and say 'yes, most of the time' and, like many things, it depends on your perspective of the situation and the way the question is phrased."

David's voice sounded like the whinny of a horse as he asked.

"But you go to church and everything so I thought you would know all the answers and be able say 'yes' or 'no'. Like the Bible says, 'Thou shall not' or 'Love thy neighbour', you know."

"Um!" expressed George, not really speaking but thinking aloud and trying to digest what David had said, and what was hidden inside and giving him so much pain. George stopped mid-field and just looked at the cattle gently grazing, seemingly without a care in the world.

"They are beautiful animals, aren't they?" said George. "Real show-stoppers, as if an artist had painted them. The artist has used only two colours, so the real beauty is in the design painted on them."

"Well, that's a different way of looking at a bunch of cows," muttered David.

"But that's the point. I see one thing, you see something totally different, but they are the same cows."

"Oh!" exclaimed David.

Walking a little further, George pirouetted round, dropped

on to one knee, flung his arms wide and began to sing. David took a pace backwards and just stood there catching flies, his mouth wide open! George had a good baritone voice and proffered a better than fair rendition of 'Love is a Many Splendored Thing'. David's fly-catching jaw just moved soundlessly up and down, lost for words; his face one of total bewilderment.

As George came to the end of the song, he looked at David and grinned a 'didn't I do well' grin that only a pleased-with-himself young boy would use having completed a dastardly deed successfully.

The grin seemed to release David, who roared with laughter and bowed deeply from the waist saying, "I thank you good sir, but I am already spoken for!"

The two continued to laugh together. Catching his breath, George motioned for them to sit down on the bank of the river. Sporadic gales of laughter continued as they began to calm down. George, in a calmer moment, said, "That is what I was trying to say about love and my marriage to Barbara. It is a many splendored thing."

Laughter broke out again that seemed to go on for an eternity. George began to speak again with a more serious note, but still only a hair's breadth from more raucous laughter.

"I love you David," said George.

At which point, David burst again into gales of laughter.

George continued, "I love you, but not in the same way as Anne loves you."

"I am glad about that George," with a rather rude gesture and look on his face.

"I also don't love you in the same way that God loves you."

David with a surprised look, "God loves me?"

"Yes, David He does," confirmed George.

"Hang on a minute, Anne loves me and you love me but

in different ways and God loves me but in a different way as well? So are you saying George there are three different types of love and not just 'love'?"

"Yep!" said George.

"But I thought love was *love*, you know the pain that makes you feel sick when you've kissed for the first time, or because your underpants feel too tight, or makes you go all weak at the knees and do stupid things when gorgeous women are around."

"I am talking about love, not lust, you dimwit," said George with an exasperated look on his face."

In a teasing way, David quipped, "Oh I thought you were going to get down to some juicy bits!"

George's eyes looked to the clear blue sky as if trying to find something to give him inspiration that would help him lift David's thoughts and the conversation from below the navel.

He continued with more composure in his voice. "So what I am saying is that there are three types of love."

David butted in. "But surely love is love?"

"Yes, and no," said George.

"Come on now, make your mind up. Are there three or is it George's imagination?"

"The answer is 'yes', although the Greeks had many words for the different facets of love."

"The Greeks?" choked David. "What have they got to do with things?"

George wagged his finger in a superior fashion and held it across his lips, indicating to David for him to be quiet and just to listen for a few moments.

"The first and most abundant love is called Agape, that's Godly love. The second is called Phelio and is more of a brotherly or sisterly love. The third is Eros, or erotic love, which is the root of the love between man and woman."

"Now we are getting down to it," said David with a big smirking grin on his face.

George just hung his head in despair, shaking it gently from side to side and whispering an incantation to the river, as if seeking some of its strength. David grinned like the proverbial Cheshire cat while George, head down and shaking, continued to whisper incantations of despair.

He continued, "God's love gives without demanding anything in return, forgives without requiring an apology, loves a person without receiving love from them, and holds no anger or grudge, even if a person hates or is ambivalent towards Him."

David interrupted, "That's a very one-sided list if you are God, giving to another without expecting anything, even love in return!"

"But that's the point. God loves each one of us and wants to have a loving relationship and give us the very best of everything He has to give. Not 'I'll love you more because you buy me flowers, do the washing-up or clean the house'! He loves us because of who we are and regardless of what we are."

"Oh!" exclaimed David. "Are you saying God loves me, no matter who or what I am and have done or may do in the future?"

"Yep! Bullseye in one."

"But I don't love Him like you do or go to church and stuff," sighed David.

"That my little friend is the whole point. God loves you regardless and will continue to love you even if you don't show any love towards Him."

A gentle calming silence fell over the pair as they ambled along, each mulling over George's words and how God's love might be an influence in their lives.

"What's pillow love George?" questioned David?

"Pillow love?" muttered George frowning. "It's Phelio love not pillow love, dummy."

"So what does it mean? What kind of love is it?" questioned David.

George's smile was generous and radiant as he looked at his little friend.

"It's the sort of love we share!" David stopped dead in mid-stride.

"Oh! I didn't think of us as in love. I thought we were just good mates and the like."

"We are!" came the emphatic reply. "You see, Phileo love is 'mates' love' and a lot more besides." David's "oh!" had an air of uncertainty about it, as did his head down posture and slow stumbling gait.

"Phileo love, like Agape love, is a giving sort of love between two or more people."

"Two or more people? That sounds like an orgy to me!" said David sarcastically.

"No, it is not!" was George's sharp response. "The reason it can be two or more is because it could equally be called 'comrade's love'. You know, the sort you see between military personnel or friends that have taken their simple friendship a step further. All parties give to and take from the joint relationship in equal measure. They enjoy a trust shared, time together, sadness together and the comradeship of just doing things together. As the relationship deepens, there is nothing each wouldn't do or sacrifice for the other, even sacrificing their own life, which is why it could be equally called 'mates or comrades love'."

"But how do you manage the sexual side of the relationship?" asked David.

"Generally you don't need to because the sexual side is not a part of the relationship as different priorities and motives draw the group together. Like you and me!"

As David walked deep in thought, he kicked at the grass aimlessly with each stride as if it was a football. He had his head down, concentrating on what his feet were doing while mumbling to himself and trying to unravel, understand and grasp the concepts George had spoken of. Still, with an uncertain mind and a sharp edge to his voice, David asked, "What is the third type of Greek love then?"

"Eros is the title they gave the third type of love," responded George, with a much gentler, compassionate tone of voice.

"Eros!" exclaimed David. "As in erotic and good old rumpy pumpy?"

George shook his head in despair.

"No! It's not just the good old rumpy pumpy, as you put it."

"Well, what is it then?" interrupted David.

George remained quiet.

"Well, what is it then?" came the insistent question. George took a coin out of his pocket, flicked it into the air, caught it and, slapping it on to the back of his hand, said, "Heads or tails?"

David, looking blankly at George, responded automatically, "Heads!"

George looked under his hand at the coin and, showing David, said, "It's tails!"

David nodded in agreement and looked at George expectantly for some great revelation or exposition on love and the relevance of the coin. George remained quiet, deep in thought. After a few moments that seemed an eternity to David, George looked directly at him, eye to eye.

"Eros love, human love, has two sides just like the coin.

One side is self-satisfying, takes what it wants with little regard for the other person. The act of love making, for instance, becomes more carnal sex at the other's expense, sometimes cruelly satisfying a base urge. On the opposite side of the coin, the same act can be a beautiful joining of mind, heart and body. Each participant giving, receiving, encouraging and being attentive to the other's needs.

"Widening the perspective a little, one person gives flowers on Valentine's Day and other similar times, but only when required and with minimal love in their heart. The other gives flowers at any time just because the love in the heart prompts the giving of a gift. The influence of this giving love, like the ripples on a pond reach out to all areas, all parts of the relationship, making it special in many different ways to each partner."

David looked at George wistfully as they continued to amble along the river bank, stopping and sitting down in the corner of the big field.

"I think I understand the last two; 'mates' love' being one type and 'love of spouse' being another. I am not sure about loving God or the term 'the giving love' in marriage, but I think I understand what you mean in the difference between that and carnal love. God's love still seems very one-sided, more like the carnal from God's perspective! Why does He love me even though I don't love Him? If He does love me, why doesn't He make things right and stop the bad things happening?"

George lifted his hand in submission. "That's a question many a theologian would like the answer to."

"So what is the answer? What is God's love like and why doesn't He make life simpler with fewer of the 'thou shalt nots'."

"The only answer I can give David; is that God's love is the very best of love, especially the 'giving love'. God loves you with all his heart and wants you to love Him in similar fashion. Not because you feel you need to, or have to, or think it's the right thing to do. He wants you to love Him from your heart because your heart and mind are in love with Him without any ulterior motives, peer pressure or pressure from God. You see, God does love you David, of that I know for certain. His love is a real love that embodies the best of Eros and Phileo love but goes much deeper into a spiritual love that is even more special."

David, with a somewhat frustrated voice, asked, "If God is God and all powerful why doesn't He just say, 'David love me with all your heart,' and I would?"

"That's a very black and white question, a bit like the cows, but the answer may not always be that simple. God wants a two-way loving relationship, not one that is prescriptive or forced."

David sighed, shaking his head in mock despair.

"You see, we have what is called 'free will' and that creates a million shades of grey, blurring the edges between black and white."

"What do you mean by 'free will' George? God is all powerful, we do what He wants us to do and we don't really have any choice!"

"That's the point, we do. God loves us and He wants us to love Him back, freely, not because we have to."

David frowned, "But God said, 'Thou shalt not', to Adam and Moses and gave the Jews loads and loads of laws."

"Those laws, in the main, were for their well-being and subsequently our well-being." George continued. "It is like your mum saying to you each day, 'wash behind your ears.' It is a law, but one for your benefit. The result of not washing behind your ears is you get dirty and eventually get skin infections."

"That's a fair cop," said David. "Mum was always saying that and many others besides."

"The irony is that God gave us the free will to choose what we do, but most of all to love Him or not. He is not a dictator, just a loving father trying to care for and do the best for his children."

David snapped, saying, "So you are telling me I am a child of God now as well as being loved by Him!"

"Yep," said George.

David just sat there not saying anything, just tugging at the grass angrily and throwing it into the river.

George continued with a more gentle tone. "It's not that hard to understand really. God loves us and wants the best for us. He loves us and His love wants us to love Him back, not because we have to but because we want to. That's the real purpose of the free will, the ability to choose to love God or not. In simple terms, as a Christian I have chosen to love God not because I go to church each week or am expected to for social reasons, or because God loves me, but because I, George, love God. It's a real love, much like mine for Barbara, but it is also a spiritual love that is unconditional, without any requirements or limits of any kind and can be, and is, in God a sacrificial love giving everything He holds dear to encourage me and you."

Both sat silently looking at the river and the insect life that abounded around the water's edge. David sighed, thought about speaking before turning his attention back to the river and the bald patch of earth that was appearing under his left hand.

The two friends just sat looking at the beauty all around, each deep in their own thoughts, until heavy footfalls and heavy breathing reminded them that they were not alone in the field. Their quietness had strengthened the resolve of a curious cow, that had wandered across the field to see what these two walkers were doing sat for so long by the river. Two heads spinning around in unison startled the cow, which jumped involuntarily. Snorting, it ambled off to join its comrades. George and David looked at each other, smiled, and then laughed as the air of uncertainty that had developed receded as quickly as the cow receded across the field.

David asked George to run the whole love bit past him simply just one more time so he could understand and what the rest of it all meant.

"OK!" said George. "Love of Anne – erotic plus nicer bits, but with many limitations. No dinner: no love!"

David smiled at the thought of this.

"Love of me – Phileo – has different limitations, especially when I am being a pompous pain in the butt! Love from and with God – Agape – unconditional love without any limitations. God loves us whether we love Him or not."

Punching George playfully on the arm, David said, "Put like that it sounds easy and very simple. Why could you not have said it like that earlier?"

George laughed, saying, "Come on you shrimp, it's time to get walking again. You owe me at least one pint for that lesson!"

Chapter 2

In a State?

The two friends set off along the river bank chatting amiably about the world, the price of fish and anything else that came to mind. As they passed by a quiet part of the river, David stopped and exclaimed, "Did you see that?"

"See what?" responded George.

"That bird coming out of the water with a fish in its mouth!"

"No, and birds have beaks not mouths," retorted George, forgetting his promise to be kind and loving.

"I know that," said David frustrated.

"So where is it, eagle eye?" questioned George.

"It's on the lower branches of that big tree on the other side of the river, and it has just whacked the fish's head on the branch!"

George, trying to smile and be generous, said, "OK, OK, give me a clue. Which big tree it is out of the ten or so that are on the far bank?"

"Oops," exclaimed David. "It's that one," pointing at a mature hawthorn. "The lower branch on the left."

George followed the line of the outstretched arm and pointing finger towards the tree. George studied the tree for some moments but could see nothing. Suddenly, a flash in the tree caught his eye, sharpening his vision to one spot and, as if by magic, his eyes had been given binoculars as an iridescent blue bird came sharply into focus. Both men just stood transfixed

14

as the little bird stunned the fish again by hitting its head against the tree, then, with a deft flick of the bird's head the fish vanished, head first down the throat of the bird.

"Did you see that!" exclaimed David. "What a beautiful bird and what a beakful to swallow whole."

George, unsure, said, "I think that is a kingfisher, by all its beautiful blue feathers."

"Yes it is," confirmed David. "Isn't that amazing to see? It seemed too sparkly, like the water, when it moved?"

Both men stood motionless for a time just watching the little bird fishing and going about its daily task of cleaning its feathers.

"Time to move on," said David. "We still have a couple of miles to go, but have plenty of time." Walking on, eyes and ears now tuned to the super sensitive range, they both looked around at the beauty of the wilder river areas and the managed countryside of the farm fields. Flowers to the whispery clouds in the sky were all documented, chatted about and filed in the wonder of the day.

David seemingly took one of the whispery clouds out of the sky when he asked George,

"Do you think divorce is right?"

George looked at David with a quizzical look. "Where did that come from?"

"Oh, I was just thinking of Brian and Pam and what may happen."

"Sadly, divorce is the most likely outcome, but it may be for the best," responded George.

David looked at him with eyes wide open, with an air about him that said, "I do not believe what you are saying."

"For the best?" he repeated again with greater emphasis, "For the best? I thought you were supposed to be a Christian, an 'until death us do part' sort of person! How can you say divorce is for the best if you believe what is in the Bible and said at a marriage ceremony?"

"It depends on the reasons why and the journey that the couple have taken in their marriage," responded George in a quiet, sympathetic tone of voice.

David snapped back, "But the Church, the Bible says no exceptions. It's 'till death, in sickness and in health' with no get out of jail free card. Once you have signed the register, that's it, for life."

George said nothing, just looked at the beauty that was all around.

"Well?" demanded David.

George looked at him; eyes more like letter box slits with tiny, laser-powered diamonds at their centre trying to drill into David's mind to understand, to locate his hurt, his anger.

"Love is 'a many splendored thing' with many facets, as are the other emotions that play a part in any human relationship," said George.

"So what! Are we not duty-bound by the promises we make to make the best of any marriage situation, good or bad? There is no flexibility, no 'facets' in thou shalt not!" retorted David with a snarl in his voice.

George just ambled on, seemingly ignoring David's outburst and hoping he would cool down and discuss rather than shout and be dogmatic.

David's tone, like a wildcat, snarled, "Well are you deaf?"

With a curt tone to his voice, Gorge said, "No, I just need time to think and for you to be less obnoxious and more the lovable chap you are!"

David stopped, causing George to have to do the same, a couple of steps later and turn around to face him. With a very dejected, quiet voice, David apologized.

George, in a quiet loving voice, responded, "I don't know what's biting your butt, but something about Brian's marriage problem has really got you rattled. Just give me a little time to collect my thoughts, then we can talk."

The two walked on in a sullen silence, all senses now closed down. The joys and beauty they had seen only minutes before now lost, a distant memory. Seemingly in the near empty blue sky, a solitary black cloud shaded and shrouded the two travellers from all the glories around them.

"George, I am sorry for my outburst. It is just that I am not sure what to do about the whole situation. Everything screams that it's wrong and yet...."

David paused, lost for words. He continued, "I know you go to Church and believe in God, but how do you balance the 'till death us do part' and 'thou shalt not commit adultery' or 'thou shalt not covert'. Should you not be dead set against what is happening and 'condemning' Brian, Pam and someone else, or at least one of them? It just seems as though you, the Church, God, the whole shooting match, have double standards and change the rules to suit the situation or yourself!"

George's face lit up with a big smile, but before he could speak David intervened.

"OK what's the big grin for? What do you find so funny?"

George's face continued to smile as he said, "Thank you, it's not often I am put in the same sentence as God, let alone having the same standards as Him!"

David laughed, "I see what you mean!"

George started to speak, "Your questions are very deep and profound and many have no real hard and fast answers."

David groaned as though his worst fears were being realized.

"Don't give up yet my little friend. There is, I believe, light in the tunnel of love."

David groaned even louder, crying, "Cut out the corn, it's too much for me."

George continued, "I'll start with an easier part, divorce and the Bible."

David's eyes popped open as if a million pound note had just crossed his vision.

"That's an easier part?" he questioned.

George continued to smile, "It is because the Bible says that divorce is permitted under certain circumstances, the main one of which is adultery. The sad thing is that it was male biased so the man could divorce an adulterous wife, but it was less easy for a woman to divorce an adulterous husband. That comes from the fact it was a patriarchal society, male dominated."

"So why the great 'till death us do part' bit that everyone seems to go on about?" asked David.

"Those words are really a way of saying the marriage contract is not a short-term one, it is for as long as possible. The marriage is not a one-night stand but a commitment between two people to stay together for as long as possible. For some that is a lifetime, for others, however, and sadly so, the problems of life get in the way and drive a wedge between the two, causing them to eventually split."

David, with a little force in his voice, said, "But a split is a split for whatever reason, are they not wrong in the eyes of God?"

"Yes," said George.

Before he could continue, David interjected, "I rest my case milord. Divorced for whatever reason and you are in trouble with God. Hellfire here you come!"

"Don't jump the gun David, God's not all doom and gloom. He has a loving side and cares for all His children. That's you and me by the way, plus several billion more."

"Me!?" questioned David. "You are still insisting that God loves me!"

"Yes you, you great numb brain," said George. He continued, "No one knows what goes on between two people when behind closed doors. As a for-instance, violence, physical or verbal, is not usually on public display. You see the marks afterwards or hear about the scars inside but you rarely see the punch or hear the bitter words. Over the years, if reconciliation fails to achieve harmony, love runs out or the pain becomes too great and the only real option left is divorce. The similar pathway is often followed by a multitude of other reasons that cause a relationship to falter and eventually break down."

"So who is to blame in a situation like that? Who is in the wrong?" questioned David with accent on "who is to blame".

"One person may be to blame, but it is often a combination of flaws on both sides that leads one person to 'draw stumps' and say 'I have had enough'," continued George. "This may be especially true if promises of change are not kept. New promises are then not believed, making trust harder to find so that the relationship can continue successfully."

"That, in part, I can understand, but what about when someone else is involved, the sort of breakdown you are talking about does not apply then? Surely then two people are at fault, especially the partner who is having the affair!?" queried David.

"On the face of it, you are right; the partner having the affair is in the wrong."

"So I am right then!" interjected David.

"Oh, yes on the face of it you are right David, but what about the time leading up to the adultery. Why did the partner feel the need to find companionship outside the marriage?"

"That could be any number of reasons," said David frustrated by the way the discussion seemed to be going.

"My point exactly! The reasons can be as many as the hairs on your head because each relationship is unique and therefore different, special in its own way and yet vulnerable to attack from forces from within and outside the relationship."

"I think I see," said David. "But I am not wholly convinced, because the words used by the Church are definite, black and white. Don't you get excommunicated or something? You know, sent to Coventry, if you are caught."

George smiled and said, "As a general rule, not any more although it depends on the circumstances and how other people around you feel."

"How do you mean?" questioned David.

"Well!" said George. "Some people will try to balance what has happened, to look beyond the immediate foreground of the picture into the background. People like that may perceive the underlying problems in the marriage and be willing to be gentle, loving and help both partners through a difficult time. Other people, sadly, can be very dogmatic, take one side or the other and be very black and white, as you say. Through their lack of understanding they can excommunicate a person or at least make their life intolerable in their community making the pain of separation even more painful."

The two friends continued to walk along the river bank, each deep in thought. Their silence was broken when a voice called out to George. Looking up they could see no one. The voice called out again, this time they both realized that it was from the opposite bank of the river. A waving arm focused their eyes on Pete, an acquaintance of George. After a brief discussion across the river, they agreed to meet a little further up the river where giant stepping stones crossed bank to bank.

George and David waited and watched nervously as Pete made his unsteady way across the stones. Pete leapt to the steep river bank with great vigour but missed his footing on the river dampened grass and slid towards the beckoning water. David moved like a bullet out of a gun towards Pete. Digging one heel in the bank as he grabbed Pete's hand, he arrested his slide. Pete's feet, however, continued to side. He fell forward, hitting the bank with a grunt. One wayward foot made it all the way back into the cool waters. George joined David and in similar fashion dug a heel in the bank and took Pete's other hand. With a one, two, three count they pulled Pete to safety on dry ground.

"Thanks, both of you. That was a near miss don't you think!" exclaimed Pete.

David, without thinking, said, "You need to practice your standing jumps or next time if you can't walk on water you will be in the water up to your knees!"

Pete laughed in a good natured way.

"Thanks for that advice, I'll try and remember that next time."

David was caught off guard by Pete's light-hearted and quick response and went a little pink in the face. George didn't help either, sniggering like a young boy behind David's back and making him feel even more embarrassed.

Pete looked him straight in the eye and said, "I was never very good at walking on water without help!"

David's jaw turned into a fly-catcher again, moving up and down soundlessly just trying to hide his embarrassment. George, however, roared with laughter, which soon set the other two off. After formal introductions, apologies given and accepted and an invitation for Pete to join them for lunch, the trio headed off towards the Black Swan.

Chapter 3

Route Map

The three men ambled along chatting amiably about the weather, life the universe and a million other things.

Pete swung his arm in an exaggerated gesture towards the river saying, "Isn't that beautiful, so clear, so full of life, a joy to any fisherman's heart."

George smiled, agreeing with Pete, and said, "I am glad I live by this river now and not 150 years ago. With the mill race and its industries working flat out this would have been a very different river."

"I agree!" said Pete. "It's a shame when good ideas and intentions get distorted and the poorer attributes of mankind take over."

"Pete, what do you mean by 'poorer attributes of mankind'? Surely all that went on here was progress, which led to the industrial revolution and the world as we know it today?" queried David.

Pete smiled, saying, "How long have you got to answer a question like that?"

Relaxing in Pete's company, David's quick dry wit was slowly coming to the fore as he retorted, "About a mile and three quarters is all before we reach the Duck!"

"Well said that man," Pete responded laughingly. "It's nice to hear you being you and not as tight as a bow string."

"Never mind his bow string," responded George

sarcastically. "Wait till you get to the Duck, then you'll see how tight his purse strings are!"

David yelped as is if prodded by a pin. "That's not fair you know. I always pay my round, unlike some who go to the loo when it's their turn."

"What do you mean? I always buy my round," snapped George.

"Can I just say something before someone's head gets well and truly bitten off?"

"Yes!" they responded to Pete's question.

Pete continued, "David, you asked me what the 'poorer attributes of mankind' were? Listen to the two of you and you can hear the beginnings of selfishness, jealousy, greed and anger all over a round of drinks!"

George ashamedly said, "I, we, are sorry Pete. We just get carried away at times. I know it's only a little thing but our colleague Bill can be a real pain for not paying his round. Bill's attitude winds us up and gets us down."

David was busy nodding his head in agreement like a 'nodding dog' in the rear window of a car on a cobbled street.

"I see!" said Pete. So many things can start out with the best of intentions, like having a pint with your mates. But, when one becomes selfish and evades buying his round it causes hurt and resentment in the others. If this hurt, like a wound, is left to fester it will poison the relationship and maybe even the person who feels the hurt most keenly."

David piped up, "So how do you tell a person to put his hand in his pocket?"

"That depends on the relationship you have and the type of love you share with the other person." Smiling inwardly, Pete continued, "You see, there are three types of loving relationships."

Almost in unison two right hands went up in the air like a policeman stopping traffic. George looked at David, then at Pete, saying, "That's incredible, we were only talking about that as we were walking along, before we met you at the stepping stones!"

Silence once again descended on the three, allowing the beauty of the river, its scents and sounds, to filter in under the black cloud that still seemed to hover above them. Pete asked them to tell him what they had been talking about that involved the three understandings of love. Jointly, as if playing ping-pong, George and David batted the subject backwards and forwards, telling Pete about their journey along the river bank.

"So what started such a wonderful discussion? What was the spark?" questioned Pete.

George pointed at David. "I cannot tell a lie, it was him. He started it asking if I loved Barbara!" David, head hanging down and stubbing his shoe toe in the grass, embarrassed, mumbled, "Yes."

Pete looked at George and asked, "Do you love Barbara?"

"Yes I do!" he responded with great conviction.

Pete's eyes met David's, who responded, "I suppose so," to the unasked question. "Do you know what prompted the discussion, as there is often an underlying reason?"

"No," said George. "I think it was just one of those things."

Pete continued, "That's OK. Many a time things do just evolve, like being on a journey without a planned route. It's a journey of exploration, a mystery tour so to speak, I like those, because nothing is definite all things are possible and the end can be whatever you want it to be, a surprise, something new or a continuation of what has gone before. I remember years ago, as if it was yesterday, having plans and hopes in my head, then everything got turned upside down. My journey then seemed to have come to a full stop. Everything lost. I was heartbroken. But that is when I started the mystery journey. I had no route map, no idea of the route or the destination. I still don't! What a journey it has been, thrilling. It's like meeting and talking with you two here on the banks of this beautiful river."

Pete's joy of his surroundings, new friendships and his love of life seemed to radiate and infect both George and David, making them both feel at ease.

"Come on you two," said Pete, grinning like a Cheshire cat. "We can talk of love and how the world was created as we walk; I am getting ready for a drink."

David and George smiled at each other, the dark cloud slowly lifting, turned and followed Pete as they set off once again along the river pathway.

Pete was humming a nonsense tune to himself when David asked, "What was it on your journey that started your mystery journey? The two seem at odds with each other. Surely life is just one long grind of a journey."

"Oh no!" said Pete. "Life is not just a long grind. That would be terrible. We have ups and downs, good days and not so good days, health and illness. They are all part of the tapestry of our lives. The big challenge is how you look at and work through the not so good days and times, be as positive as you can so you get the best from what is there."

"Sounds easy when you say it like that, but it's not so easy when you are deep in the mire," responded George, with David doing his nodding dog act again in agreement.

"I didn't say it was easy! It's not! But if you can find the positive, the joy, the beauty in the situation then life changes from being wholly negative to something positive. The situation may not be thorns and thistles or sweet-scented violets but a fragrant mixture so the negative becomes bearable and, in some cases, takes on a beauty of its own."

"How do you move from one to the other and find the beauty you speak of when you are in the middle of pain and hurt?" questioned David.

"How I move, how George moves, how you move from one to the other is a personal journey. I cannot give you a map or a set of instructions because I am not you. All anyone can do is give helpful encouragement and to be there alongside, to listen, to help and support but not to condemn or give too much advice saying you need or must do this or that because they have their interpretation of the situation and their way of coping with it, and is not necessarily yours."

David, George and all around seemed to be holding their breath, listening intently as Pete continued.

"I had to travel that journey when I thought I lost my best friend. All my hopes and dreams dissolved in front of me."

"Oh Pete, I am so sorry. I had no idea. I didn't mean to drag up the past like that," wailed David.

"It's OK David, that point in my life was only the end of the beginning," said Pete, "The mystery journey was then about to begin. You see, although I thought I had lost my best friend, I hadn't, I had only lost what I could see. What I got back, as I began the mystery journey, was an even closer friend who, in so many ways, became part of me and I part of him. I had no idea where I was going, what I was going to. I just trusted in his guiding words."

"That sounds very complex and convoluted," said George, trying to wrestle with what had been said.

"It's not easy to understand, I grant you, but time, trust and personal experience often overcome the logical thoughts and ways of the brain."

George grinned, looked at David and said, "First, you need

a brain with logical thoughts and ways!"

"Cheeky monkey!" was David's response, along with long belly laughter all round.

The trio stopped near a set of rapids downstream from the old mill race, watching the water bubble and boil playfully as it surged over the rocks to seemingly stop at the bottom of the rapids in the sluggish waters of a deep pool. In the water between the rapids and pool, brown trout hovered, heads into the current, tails lazily providing the power to prevent them slipping back into the deep dark pool.

"Aren't they beautiful?" said George. "Effortless power."

"I used to catch them as a kid," said David. "My dad taught me how to tickle them and they don't half taste good when they are freshly caught!"

"That's typical of you, a real misspent youth. I'll bet you used to snare rabbits as well," George intimated in a very lofty tone of voice.

"Actually no!" retorted David. "I used to borrow my dad's shotgun and shoot them. It was quick and painless. Which is not what I would like to do to you right now!" said David with a glint in his eye.

Pete just gloried at the fish below and smiled at the pair of them enjoying friendly banter.

"Pete, how does your route map relate to love and is there any basic map written down anywhere? At the moment it all seems very will-o'-the-wisp, without substance and difficult not so much as to comprehend, but to get hold of, to believe!" asked George.

"That's the nub of it, the believing! But I understand your need for something you can hold, read or write down," Pete continued. "Your route map is yours and yours alone, no one else's. The three forms of love are the way in which you interact with other people and nature in general along the way. The best guide is in Holy Scripture and was carved by Moses on tablets of stone."

"Do you mean the Ten Commandments?" inquired David.

A nervous smile lined his face as he looked for, hoped for, affirmation to his all too quick response.

"Yes!" said Pete with an encouraging smile. "But, like many things, they have a dual interpretation."

David, like the trout, rose to the bait and snapped, "How can 'Thou shalt not' have a dual meaning? It's as plain as any nose God was saying, 'don't do this or that or you will be punished!'"

Pete spoke quietly in gentle tones when he said, "That is a very dogmatic and bitter viewpoint of something that was given out of love. Given to help firstly, a young nation; then through them, all mankind, to help them interact with God and with each other."

David's hackles flared up once again. Pete's seemingly gentle words of explanation touched a raw nerve and he retorted with venom.

"But the Ten Commandments are all 'don't do this' or 'don't do that'. There is no love in them! They are all punishment laws and all the laws we have made through the centuries follow the same pattern! There is no love in them, only condemnation of the person who has done wrong!"

Pete looked at David with a mixture of sadness and love, trying to reach out to him to ease the turmoil, pain, anger and guilt inside. As he looked, Pete could see great barriers being erected around David to self-protect. To keep out strangers, but also to keep out truth and love. Pete tried to reach out to David, to take his hand but, like a young child, David turned away as if trying to hide in a corner.

"David, when you were a young child your mother loved you and taught you many things."

David looked at Pete with a wary eye as if trying to analyze whether he was friend or foe. All he could see was a kindly face with eyes that sparkled and seemed to penetrate deep into his heart.

Pete continued, "Your mum taught you how to use a knife and fork, to sit up and eat in a polite manner."

"Yes she did. What of it?" David spat out as if the words had a bitter taste.

"Well the Ten Commandments are God's way of telling you how to use a knife and fork; how he wants us to interact with Him and each other," Pete said gently.

George looked up from watching the trout.

"Come on you dimwit, that makes it clearer than crystal. Can you not see? Your mum will have said 'don't put your knife in your mouth' or 'use your fork as a fork and not a mechanical digger' and I've seen you do that often enough. They are all, in a sense, negative laws that have a positive outcome. They teach by saying 'no' as much as God saying 'thou shalt not' is only a posh way of saying 'no'!"

David just scowled at George. The three men just stood in silence watching the river with each wrapped up in their own thoughts, time endless, tranquility flowing all around them; the river seemingly washing away the hard thoughts and doubts as it had the industrial waste in bygone times. It was as though the river had decided it was time to speak and broke the silence as a large trout surged clear of the water, mouth agape. At the top of its arc, the trout's mouth snapped shut around a mayfly, before re-entering the river with a splash many a competitive diver would have been pleased to make.

"Did you see trout?" exclaimed George. "What a belter.

That was breakfast, dinner and supper in one fish."

Jolted from his dark thoughts by the fish, David looked at Pete saying, "I have got the wrong idea about what God wants and the Ten Commandments, haven't I?"

"Sadly, like many, you have David, but all is not lost because My Lord is always willing to teach us, to forgive and help us on our journey through life."

With a quizzical look, David responded with a hushed voice, almost childlike, "You sound as though you have experienced this 'God' and His teaching in your life personally!"

Pete's smile lit up his face, radiating from every corner, and his eyes glowed white hot as if David was looking into a blast furnace. With a reflective tone and a smile better than any clowns, Pete simply said, "I have!"

George broke the intimate silence with a practical comment, "Come on you two, time to walk or we'll not get last orders tonight let alone this afternoon."

Laughing, they turned to continue up river towards the mill race. As they walked against the flow of water, it was as if the river was rolling the rocks around in their hearts and washing away the rubbish in their minds, opening the way for other possibilities.

Chapter 4

The Greatest

"Pete?" questioned George. "You know the order of the Ten Commandments. Is there any reason why they are in that order?"

"How do you mean George?"

"Well, you know the first four, I think it is, talk about God the one and only and keeping Sunday precious and such like; then the last ones talk about sex and stealing!"

David piped up, "Yep, God was dead set against sex in the 'thou shalt not' department!"

Pete laughed at the two of them.

"What a pair of hardboiled egg heads you two are!" he continued. "Yes, there are Ten Commandments and, yes, the first four are about how we should relate to God; the final six are about how we should relate to each other. And no, God is not against sex, just the misuse of it."

David, with a silly grin on his face and a raunchy note in his voice, butted in, "Oh goody, God's not against sex so we can have orgies tonight, with wine, 'cos I know Jesus was OK with wine!"

George roared with laughter, but went suddenly quiet when he realized Pete was not with them. Looking around, George saw Pete a couple of paces back heading towards the river once again. The two friends looked at each other and, without a word, raced after Pete, who was now by the river bank.

When they caught up, George apologized to Pete.

"We are sorry, aren't we David? We didn't mean to be rude or flippant about the subject."

David nodded his head in agreement.

"But with our thoughts we just got things a little… er, off balance."

Pete just gazed up into the branches of an oak tree, seemingly lost in wonder.

"That's not a problem," said Pete. "I just wanted to show you this tree."

David looked at the tree, eyes open extra wide trying to penetrate the lattice work of leaves to see what was special.

Finally he said, "It's a big tree I grant you but what is so special about it because I can't see anything different about this tree?"

"It's the way you look at it, like looking at black and white painted cows," commented Pete. George and David looked at each other with curious expressions on their faces and a myriad of questions flying through their minds.

"How do you know about the cows? When David and I were talking, you were on the other bank."

Pete just smiled. "I know many things, one of which is that sound travels easily over still waters."

"Oh!" said George.

Pete continued, "The tree is beautiful, so vibrant so full of life, a world in miniature."

"Come on Pete, I know it's a beautiful tree but a miniature world is getting a bit over the top," retorted David.

"Not really David," he continued. "Open your mind to the possibilities, to the insects, the birds, the animals that live and die in and around this tree."

"That's not a world," snapped David.

"Ah, but it is!"

"No it's not!" interrupted David.

Pete continued, "The tree is as much a world to its residents as this planet Earth we live on is to us in the universe."

David frowned not really understanding, but not sure how or what to ask. "The tree has many tiny creatures that live their whole life in that tree, so to them it is their world. They have no idea about the mill race or your house, just this lovely tree. There are billions of stars and planets in the universe, any one could support life. That life may live, work and die without knowing of planet Earth or David and George that live in Nether Padley."

George had a big, generous, wide smile on his face as David said simply, "Oh, I see."

"The creatures in the tree, the tree itself, live year by year, season by season in a sort of balance that allows each to flourish, grow, procreate and then ultimately die. They have no rules written down, just the rules 'hardwired' into their genetic being."

"Tosh!" exploded David, "Hardwired rules, rubbish. I suppose you'll be saying we are hardwired as well. The only thing that's hardwired is a computer!"

George shook his head in a sad, reflective mode before saying, "You know David, at times you don't listen and go off half-cocked. We have things that are in our make-up that are, as Pete put it, 'hardwired', like standing on two feet."

David just looked at the ground and mumbled incomprehensible words to himself. In a quiet soft voice Pete continued, "It's OK David. When your mind is in turmoil, uncertain of what to do, it is natural to fight back to protect yourself and prevent others from getting too close."

David just scowled, but could not meet Pete's penetrating, loving eyes.

"David! The final six commandments are 'statements of doing', but they are also like chapter headings in a book. God, in His love, has given us those headings. We have the free will to interpret those headings as we will, if you like, to write the story of and in the chapter."

"Ah!" said George, "I think I understand, that's quite a nifty way of putting it Pete."

Pete just smiled.

"OK clever clogs, so why does one thief get put in jail, another get off with a caution and another get community service? Answer me that!" David spat.

"That's the point, that's the part of the chapter we have written. God said 'Don't steal', we took that as our title for a chapter and filled it with laws and punishments on stealing. We wrote down a great long list of different types of stealing and an even longer list of punishments."

George became very animated with great arm gestures and exaggerated pronunciation as he pronounced judgement.

"So you see, for each act of stealing a judge and jury would decide from a whole range of punishments how much to punish a person, if at all." Having finished, George just smiled smugly.

"That's all very well," whined David. "But not all the commandments carry the same status. Some carry a greater penalty than others."

"In God's eyes they are all the same, there is no hierarchy. The penalty, the cost of each one is paid for by the same price," Pete said in a gentle, almost whispering voice.

"What a load of rubbish and you know it! If I steal or murder someone people will forgive me and help me to be 'rehabilitated' into society. If I sleep with my neighbour's husband the same would be true. If, however, I sleep with my neighbour's wife and commit adultery that's totally different. Then there is no rehabilitation and I am condemned and branded for years. Some people even lose their jobs. Where is the fairness in that?"

"David, I know that is not fair, but it's not God that is handing out the punishment, it's humankind, society in general and the local people around you. They are the ones who judge and pass sentence, often without knowing the 'whys' and 'wherefores', not God. For those people who love God and are truly sorry for their faults, their errors, their transgressions, call it what you will, their sentence, their time in prison if you like, has been served for them!"

Pete continued to look at David with a sad expression yet with eyes that seemed to be filled and flooded with compassion towards him instead of tears.

"Pete?" questioned George, "Didn't Jesus, when he was asked about the commandments, say something like, 'Love God and love your neighbour' were the greatest commandments?'"

A triumphal grin spread across Pete's face as wide as the Cheshire cat's, yet with a loving warmth about it.

"Yes!" he said.

Peace seemed to descend over the three as they digested all that had been said. David's tone, much softer, asked, "Pete, if what George has just said is true, which is the greatest, to love God or love my neighbour?"

Pete just remained quiet for a few moments looking at the river as it danced over the rocks on its long journey to the sea. Finally, he posed a question to David, "Which do you think is the most important to God?"

"I suppose to love God is the most important to Him!"

"On the nose!" said Pete.

"Oh!" gasped David in confusion, "I thought it was going to be a trick question."

Pete took a half-step sideways and put his arm gently but firmly around David's shoulders before speaking.

"You, David, are important to God and loved by Him!"

"All He asks is that we love Him in return. We don't have to, it's not His way to force us, we have the choice, to love Him or not."

David's voice had lost all its strident notes and became a tremulous whisper as he asked, "Are you saying God really loves me now, as I am?"

Pete's arm tightened around David's shoulder in reassurance, "Yes! He loves you now as much as He ever has, possibly more, because He knows you need His love and reassurance now more than ever."

Silence once again fell over the three friends, each deep in their own thoughts. Each looked at the scene around them. Different aspects of the natural beauty touched their hearts and minds, each finding something to wonder at.

Minutes ticked gently by before George, looking at Pete, said, "You seem very sure that God loves David and me!"

"God loves all His children, especially those that are lost or have done wrong because those are the ones that need Him most," responded Pete.

"That is the story behind the story of the lost sheep. God leaves the sheep that are protected and seeks out the one that is in need. He loves them all, but the one that is lost needs that extra bit of tender loving care. God's love is like a mother's, who lovingly tends to her son's grazed knee while she watches over her daughter playing with her dolls in the safety of the lounge."

"What a simple picture, yet profound and easy to grasp," gasped George.

The sun seemed to dance on the river with an even greater

intensity, as though they both wanted to join in the conversation. The three friends began to meander with thoughtful, but not heavy, steps on their way to the Black Swan.

Pete broke the silence. "If you love God or your neighbour, you want to please them; to do things that please them as an expression of your love. God does love you, and hopefully your neighbour will do the same in return. A love that is full does no harm because it is not in its nature. Neither of you would hurt the other because you love each other deeper than you both realize."

George stopped as though he had hit a wall,

"Excuse me, Pete!" he said with an authoritarian tone in his voice, "How do you know how much I love David and vice versa? We are just good mates and that is all we are!"

"True, but in time you will find life in all its vagaries will test your friendship, your love for each other. However, unlike me, I hope you will stand side by side without faltering through the darkest of times."

"It is a nice thought George, to think that you would stand by me. I hope what Pete says is true," said David with a thoughtful, wispy voice.

As they rounded the bend, the pathway steepened, climbing alongside the cut that once held the water wheel that powered the forge and its simple yet powerful hammers.

George looked at the crumbled buildings, saying, "It seems incredible that so much of our modern industrial world's foundations started in places like this."

"True," said Pete. "But the cost to the earth and humankind in general can be very high. Humankind is often very blinkered and sees only what it wants to see when riches, power and wealth beckon. Often we are not willing or able to step back and see the other side of the coin or the bigger picture."

"Pete! Following the coin idea; you seemed to suggest earlier that there was another side, another meaning to the Ten Commandments. Is there?" questioned David.

Pete sat down quietly on the large stone blocks that once supported the water wheel and formed the edge of the cut. Patting the blocks on either side of himself, he motioned for David and George to join him.

Chapter 5

Four into One

They sat looking at the water as it cascaded through the narrow gap where the wheel had once been. Upstream at the pond end of the cut the water was higher, held back by the narrowness of the cut. The huge volume of water from the mill pond was trying to force its way through the small gap like a crowd of people through a door. Once released from the gap, the water raced away as if trying not to be caught by the water still pushing through. As the water rushed under their feet it still had time to play with the moss and weeds that clung to the stone walls. The water gurgling and bubbling seemed to be saying to the vegetation, "Come and join us on our journey, come with us!"

As Pete sat there at peace; tranquility seemed to descend all around. Even the cascading water seemed hushed as if waiting for his words, not wishing to miss one syllable. As they continued to sit, an air of tranquility seemed to form a bubble over and around them; time did not stop, it was now of no importance. Neither of the friends spoke; they, lost in their own world, waited quietly, patiently. Pete drew in a gentle breath, ready to speak. That almost inaudible act was the trigger, the signal, for all within the bubble fell silent. Ears cocked and straining, eyes fixed on the middle-seated figure, many more creatures than the two human ones were prepared, listening.

Pete turned, facing George.

"George, you are a man of the Church. What do the first four commandments say?"

The colour in George's face drained away as if it had become one with the rushing waters of the race as they sped on their journey.

"Err…," began George, "I can't remember them word for word, but I'll try."

David sniggered till Pete's hand rose but a centimetre; all went quiet.

"They say there is only one God and we are not to worship any other God. We are not to make any idols and worship them. We are not to swear by or misuse God's name and we are not to work on the seventh day and to keep that day holy. I think that's the basics of the first four."

George looked toward Pete for encouragement. Pete just smiled and nodded. Then, turning to David, he enquired?

"Are there any bits he has missed out David?"

David just sat there, his face translucent, jaw moving silently, but no words came out. Like a fish out of water, he gulped in a great quantity of air before speaking in a squeaky, childlike voice.

"Doesn't it say no one should work on a Sunday, including the animals?"

"Well done, yes it does."

Buoyed-up by the encouragement, David continued. "And doesn't it say God will punish all forms of wrong doers for many generations, you know bring down fire and brimstone and the like?"

Pete's smile continued to be warm, friendly and encouraging.

"Part of what you say has an air of truth in it. It is a little jumbled, but no matter."

"What do you both think the first four commandments are

all about?" continued Pete.

With a little frown on his face, George replied, "Isn't it about our relationship, you know how we should behave towards God."

"Yes!" responded Pete, "But there is so much more! My people had just escaped from Egypt, a land of many gods. Yahweh is passionate about his people and wanted them to love Him as He loved us."

"Yahweh?" queried David.

"That's one of God's names," explained Pete. Looking at David, he continued, "It's only those that hate or turn their backs to Him that He will punish, but those that love Him will be loved in return beyond measure."

"Is the first part the fire and brimstone bit? An eye for an eye and all that, the love me or else from God?" interrupted David.

"Not quite," continued Pete. "You see, even if you hate Yahweh, say things and do things that injure His children, but then from the heart say, 'I am sorry', He will forgive you and encourage you to become one of his children. Yahweh did not want His children to continue in their old 'Egyptian' ways, worshipping Him along with other foreign gods. He wanted them to love Him as a child does a parent, from the heart, wholly and completely.

"You see, if you love someone from the heart then you will do almost anything to please them, just as a courting couple do. Yahweh is no different, He loves each of us in the same way and will go to any length to demonstrate to us His love and encourage us to love Him. To put it in one simple sentence; Yahweh loves David! Yahweh loves George! Both with all His heart, no matter what you do or say. All He hopes for is that you will love Him in return."

David, with a huge question in his voice, asked, "You are saying Yahweh loves me regardless of what I do and what I may be doing now or in the future?"

"That's right! David do you know the story of the Good Shepherd?"

"Sort of," he replied. "Didn't the shepherd lose one sheep and have to go and find it before it got killed?"

George snorted and had one of those smug 'I know the answer' smirks on his face. Pete looked at him with a gentle, patient look, saying, "And your interpretation George, is?"

"The shepherd had 100 sheep; he lost one on the drive to the evening pen. He locked up the 99 and then went to look for the one he had lost. Like all good stories, he found it, of course, and brought it home a happy man. In the same way God brings us, His committed Christian children, home because he loves us."

A wry smile crossed Pete's face. "George, why go to all the effort to recover the one sheep or child? Could the shepherd not be justified in saying that its loss was collateral damage for that day? After all he still had the 99 and could replace the one easily enough at the next lambing season? Or that there are so many children, a lost one could soon be replaced?"

George frowned.

"Or was it, is it, because the sheep and we are special to Him? We are favourites of His?"

"Sort of," responded George.

"My Lord told the story to try and demonstrate how limitless Yahweh's love is for you and me. We, His children are the sheep being led by My Lord towards Yahweh, but there are those who get lost or led astray on the journey by a tasty patch of grass. Once lost, the sheep is at the mercy of lions and brigands. If we too become lost we are at the mercy of the poorer attributes of humankind, all of which lead to a painful and nasty end."

The two friends looked at each other and grinned with thoughts of how nasty the 'nasty end' might be.

"The shepherd, however, loves all his sheep equally: they are all special to him. Once he has bedded down the 99 in a place of safety where he can leave them, he sets off to find the one. He finds the lost one and brings it home, a happy man."

"But that's what George said," interjected David.

"True, but what was missed out was the lengths to which the shepherd went to. He was happy and rejoiced to have found the one sheep. But he did not drive it home as he had the others. He picked the one up and carried it home. We are not told how far it was or how heavy the sheep was, just that the shepherd carried it home rejoicing. Yahweh's love for each of us is the same as the shepherd's love for the sheep. If we get lost in some way He will come and find us and bring us back home, guiding us, carrying us. Whatever it takes, He will do it."

"Pete, if God's love is that big how come people hate Him and reject Him?"

"David, that's a question with as many answers as the blades of grass over there on the other bank. Even my own people found it difficult to understand how much Yahweh loved them. Many generations saw practical demonstrations of Yahweh's love and even then they looked to gold, power, greed, possessions and loved them more than Yahweh. Those and many other temptations are around us daily, some easy to spot, others more subtle in the way they lead us astray."

"Pete?" questioned George. "How does this story link with the commandments as the first four seem to be commands of how we should act towards God and how vindictive He will be towards us if we do not do as He says!"

As George's words left his lips, to the listening world a pheasant gave a strangled cry as if warning of an imminent thunderbolt and Pete visibly recoiled at George's words. He just looked into the mill race, face all knotted as if the water in the race were his tears. After sitting quietly for a short while, an unseen radiance seemed to bring the colour and smile back to his face as a man sat by a coal fire.

"George, you could not be more wrong about Yahweh and His intentions and His love for the Hebrew nation and all of humankind. Don't forget, the commandments were given to the Hebrew nation just after they had been given their freedom after generations of slavery. Through all those years they had been subjected to the gods and practices of the Egyptian people. The influences of all that time, both the obvious and the subtle, would have had an effect on my people and their way of relating to Yahweh. Their ways would have become tainted with Egyptian ways and thoughts. To go from a strict and regimented life of slavery to a life of freedom without, or even with, new rules has its own problems. This 'enlightened age' of today, is no different. It has many problems to resolve. Like a pendulum in a clock, the move from one side to the other can be very marked with both poor and good results.

"Yahweh had demonstrated His love and protection freely, no 'you do this and I'll do that', towards His people before and as they left Egypt. A little later, through Moses, He gave them rules to live by concerning their relationship with Him and each other. The first commandments state the obvious in what Yahweh had done for the Hebrew people before any sense of real love toward Him had been shown by many of my nation. They sort to cleanse the nation of their slavery ways, their Egyptian ways, so that they looked only to Yahweh for all their needs. It gave them time to rest, to set aside a special day to be with Him. As to the six generations, it's a period of time. Not so much of vindictiveness, as you put it, but a time for those who hate Yahweh and work against His desires to understand His love and learn to love Him in return. Those who refuse are the ones who are lost because they walk away from Yahweh. The rules, all of them, are a gift, given through love from Yahweh to try and help a people grow into a nation. As a nation and individuals we got lost along the way from time to time but, for those who said 'I am sorry' and called for help, Yahweh was there ready and willing to help, no matter for how long or what they had done wrong.

"The same is true today for all of us. Yahweh's gift of love has not been withdrawn after all these generations. It is offered to us all, as My Lord will tell you. The words 'I am sorry', said from a penitent heart, are like the sheep's bleat of distress. The shepherd hears that call of distress, that call that says 'I am sorry', and will come to its aid, rescuing the wayward sheep, picking it up and carrying it home rejoicing because it's now safe in his care."

Chapter 6

Six Times Two

The two friends sat pondering the words of Pete and how they might relate to themselves. As they sat quietly, the natural world found its voice once again. The whispering silence that had enveloped them came bird by bird to an end. George's dangling legs waved to and fro as though he and the mill race were playing a game as the water hurried by. David, on the other hand, sat statue-like, head down with a stone-like expression that mirrored his motionless figure.

George broke the silence with an extended 'erm' before looking at Pete with sad, puppy dog eyes.

"Pete, I can understand some of what you have said about the first four commandments but how do the remainder relate to God? I have never heard that preached before!"

"That's a good question George. How on earth can we commit adultery towards or covert God's ass?" interjected David.

Pete just grinned and shook his head hangdog-like, as though seeking divine help.

"David, why did you put adultery first followed by covetousness, or desiring what is not yours?" questioned Pete.

"Because they are the most important; at least as far as most people are concerned!" offered David with a hard note in his voice.

"Wrong," said Pete playfully.

David snapped back, "What do you mean wrong? Adultery is by far the worst and therefore number one in rank, even if it's not written down as number one. Ask anybody that's committed adultery if they have been forgiven by people around them and the answer will be 'no'! Some even lose their jobs, their homes, their friends and the like. In some circles of life, even years later, the 'you committed adultery' stigma is still there. If I killed someone or stole a bucketful of money, once I'd have served my jail sentence I would be forgiven and accepted once again. Though it's true to say not by all. Church people are just as bad if not worse. They quickly condemn, judge and pass sentence without knowing all the facts, but rarely offer understanding or forgiveness."

"Hang on a minute David, that's not fair," shouted George with a high degree of frustration and exasperation in his voice. "Church people do forgive and many try to help the injured party."

"That's the point; they forgive the injured party but not the so-called adulterer."

Pete held up both hands in a sign of peace, which he re-enforced with a firmer gesture as the two men growled at each other as if they were spitting out nails from a nail gun. Peace, like an evening mist, slowly descended, covering the friends and cooling the anger within. Its feather light touch caressed twisted faces, changing them to baby smooth with a star light's glint in the eye.

Pete looked at each man with dark pools of sadness in his eyes.

"We have a long way to go on our journey together, haven't we?"

The two friends looked at Pete with quizzical expressions, not understanding the meaning of what he had said. Pete continued, "It's one of those which side of a coin questions, heads or tails? Both are linked and in a sense both are right!"

"Rubbish," spat out David. "We can't both be right."

Pete, for the first time, laid a gentle hand on David's shoulder, squeezing gently. David's head turned and both sets of eyes met and locked together like a belt in its buckle. Pete spoke directly to David's troubled mind.

"Pain, misunderstanding, guilt and anger drive many people, even if they are misplaced and unnecessary."

David's head tilted sideways, questioning yet not speaking, his face frowning, eyes locked in to Pete's.

"The final six commandments many people call the social commandments. They were put in place to help a young Hebrew nation live together in harmony, especially on their long journey to the Promised Land. That is one side of the coin and a true and good interpretation. On the other side of the coin, however, they relate to our relationship with God just as much as the first four."

George snorted like a bull that was about to bellow to the world and proclaim how wrong that claim was. Pete once again just raised a hand in a gesture of peace. Looking at George, he smiled.

"You too have many knots inside you that colour your viewpoint and stop you being the true gentle and loving man you could be! Can I continue?" questioned Pete.

They both nodded their heads slowly and very deliberately, giving consent without wanting to admit to guilt or enthusiasm for Pete to continue.

"David, if you were God…?"

George snorted in disgust.

Pete continued. "If you were God and George came and paid homage to me instead of you, what would you do?"

George laughed loudly. "I'd stuff a sock in his mouth to shut him up before zapping him with a good old-fashioned thunderbolt!" exclaimed David.

"Why would you do that?" Pete questioned.

"Because he's got a big mouth at times and he is worshipping you not me," exclaimed David.

"And another way of saying that would be to say he was doing what, asked Pete?"

Both men sat quietly deep in thought. Time ticked by, neither wanting to speak the obvious answer to Pete's question. George looked at Pete and asked, "Do you know the answer?"

"I do," replied Pete. "And so do you, but will your mind let your heart say it?"

The knuckles on George's hands went white as they gripped the stones of the mill race, indicators of the turmoil inside. After what seemed an age, George turned his head and faced Pete and David.

"I had never thought of me worshipping someone or something else as being adultery towards God. He's above all that sort of stuff, isn't he?" questioned George.

"Yahweh is," replied Pete. "He is faithful and true to His word, His promises, for all time. The sad thing is humankind is not and when we worship another god of whatever kind it causes pain to Yahweh. In a very real way, when we worship another god, object or possession, we are committing adultery against Yahweh."

The two men sat quietly looking at nothing in particular, but not wishing to look at each other or Pete. Unlike the water in the millrace, time trickled by very slowly. David was the first to draw in a breath as if about to speak, but went all pink and confused in the face as if embarrassed by his thoughts. Time continued to trickle by until David tried again.

"Pete?" questioned David in a quiet voice. "I think I can now see what you mean about committing adultery towards God, but why does He continue to love us, and what about all the other commandments?"

"I know a very dear friend who can answer that far better than me if he's about and that sort of question usually gets his attention," replied Pete with a glowing smile on his face. "The six commandments have similar natures and relate to our interaction with each other and our spiritual interaction with God."

"David! Why do you give someone close to you a gift on their birthday?" questioned Pete.

David looked at Pete with a blank but thoughtful expression.

"I suppose because I love them or have a special relationship of some kind with them."

"OK!" responded Pete. "So, how would you feel if the gift, expensive or not, was blatantly given away or thrown in the rubbish?"

"What!" exclaimed David. "That would be the last present they would get from me."

"Right! So how do you think Yahweh would feel if He gave you a gift and you did not use it, but just threw it away?"

David paused, face knotted like an old piece of rope knowing the answer, but not wishing to respond. Pete continued.

"You see, if Yahweh honours you with a gift and you don't use it or you throw it away you dishonour Yahweh as much as the person dishonours you."

David's face transformed from a knot to a caricature of himself and all forms in between as disbelief gave way to understanding.

"Does God give me gifts then?"

"Yes!" was Pete's emphatic response.

"Oh!" said David, with a mouth like a goldfish's.

"OK, Mr Know-It-All, how do we murder God then?" asked George, in a very surly, condescending voice.

"You cannot kill Yahweh directly and with your 'learnt' knowledge, you know that," answered Pete in the somewhat firmer voice of teacher to student.

George ignored Pete and pressed his question even more firmly. "So how do we murder God?"

Pete drew in a deep breath and held it for several seconds, allowing time for his nerves to settle and to regain his own composure before responding to George.

"You kill Yahweh in yourself by separating the 'you' from 'Him' with the sort of attitude you are displaying now! You squash His love in you. You flip the coin to the other side and then throw it away regardless."

George just hung his head in shame, saying nothing while David just looked at George in wonderment at what his friend had said and with such ferocity. The three men just sat looking into the cut, each deep in their own thoughts.

After what felt like an eternity, Pete continued. "You cannot kill Yahweh, but you can kill your or another person's love for Him. In killing that love, you cut yourself off and others from Yahweh and in so doing effectively kill Yahweh to that individual. It is like you saying to David, 'I don't love you anymore' and not speaking to or interacting with him. The friendship, the love you have for each other would die and in a real sense David would eventually be dead to you."

"That's definitely a different interpretation, but one I can begin to understand and certainly not one I would want to happen," said George with a much quieter tone and contrite voice.

David looked across at George who had a fragile smile on his face.

"It's OK George; I still look to you as a good mate. A bit of a dummy at times, but a good mate all the same!"

"Thanks David, but I feel a bit of a plonker at the moment. I suppose some would say I should know better!"

"Not at all George. Learn, understand and let Yahweh's love touch every fibre in your body. Settle into His hands, His arms, because they are better than the best of soft chairs that wrap around you. Let Him teach you, touch you, let Him show you how much He loves you."

"I am not sure I know how to," said George with a woeful expression on his face and a childlike pitch to his voice.

"That does not matter. What does matter is that deep in your heart you do love Him and want a much deeper, more intimate relationship with Him if only you would untie the knots the world has got you in."

"You make it sound so easy Pete. There has to be a catch or a 'thou shalt not' in the small print!"

"Now who is being a real doom and gloom dummy?" interjected David.

"You are a man of the Church. It should be easy for you, just as Pete said."

"It's all right for you smart-ass, but I want to get it right. I want my love…"

Pete cut across George's words, "'I want' puts up demanding barriers! What does Yahweh's love for you want?"

George, stunned, went into a deep silence that became as impenetrable as a fortified castle wall.

David, looking at Pete, said, "That's a very interesting idea, but how do you 'steal' from God?"

Pete's whole face grinned at David.

"You can steal from Yahweh in many ways, but I'll try and keep it easy. If you promise to give something to Yahweh and then don't you are guilty of either stealing or breaking your promise."

David's face knotted up. "How does that work?"

"Well you have made a promise to give something. By holding on to the item you have, in a sense, stolen the item by not giving to the other person. You have also broken your promise to give the item."

"That's fine, responded David, but that's still seems to be between me and another person, not God. Are you saying that promising something to God is the same as me promising something to George?"

"Yes it is! We often make promises to Yahweh privately in our hearts. We also make more public promises with our minds and lips to give, to do, to help and so on. Then, for whatever reason, we say 'no'!" If the promise has been said privately, between you and Yahweh, then only you and Yahweh know that you have broken your promise. If said publicly, all know. Often we make excuses to shroud the broken promise, but the promise has been broken.

"Oh! That's a real catch-all way of looking at it," commented David.

"The same is true when you give false testimony," responded Pete. "You make up false statements; you lie about Yahweh to another person and in doing so cause harm to their relationship with Yahweh."

"Is that the same basic idea then to stealing from God?"

"It is!" continued Pete with a smile. "If you say to your boss you have been at work on time every day and haven't, you have lied, given a false statement to him and, in a roundabout way, have stolen time from him. If, on the morning you were late, he was looking to speak to you at five past eight he will know that you have been late for at least one day. Your boss will also know that when you say, 'I have been at work on time every day,' you are lying to him. The same is true with Yahweh. You can lie to him, embellishing all your good deeds, but he knows the truth."

"So it's really a waste of time and effort even trying to lie to God then!" retorted David.

"It is!"

"So, as far as God is concerned, why bother with that law?"

"Because you can cause Yahweh great harm by lying to others about Him. If you tell a thrilling story to a young child they will believe you in their heart. The belief that story generates can be with them for many years, or even a lifetime."

"What, you mean like Father Christmas and all that?" interjected David.

Pete smiled generously at David.

"In a manner of speaking, yes! If you tell a story about Yahweh and make Him out to be the villain then the child will believe Him to be a villain. This false story can have just as much impact as the true story. The sad thing is, it may take a lifetime to encourage the child to believe the true story of Yahweh's love for each of us."

"Hmm, OK. That I think I can begin to understand. So what is covetousness all about?" inquired David.

"David, have you ever wanted something you can't have?" asked Pete.

"Yep, most people have," was David's quick response.

"How long did it take you to get over the wanting?"

"Oh, a few days, may be weeks. It depends on what it was!"

"OK," said Pete. "But what if you really wanted it deep down and that want was a burning desire inside you?"

A sadness of feeling inadequate crept across David's face.

"I don't know if I have never felt like that!"

Pete's eyes looked at David with compassion, as if searching for the truth in his heart.

"That, in essence, is the difference. You have felt desire but not the burning passion of covetousness. Desire can be used for both wrong and good purposes. The burning passion of covetousness, however, has many other emotions embedded in it."

"What are they?" interrupted David.

"It is the wanting at all costs what someone else has that is fuelled by greed and envy," replied Pete.

The three men sat quietly together thinking about what Pete had said, each drawing inspiration and their own conclusions as they looked into the mill race and at the landscape around them. After what seemed like an eternity, the silent George looked at his watch.

"Come on you two, it's time to go. I am ready for a pint and a steak pie or something."

George's comment, the thought of food, generated laughter in the trio as they nursed stiff legs and bottoms into the upright position trying to get the blood to circulate in their leg muscles. They continued on their journey.

Chapter 7

Loves Hope

Stiff legged, the trio began the final half mile or so along the river path to the Black Swan chatting amiably, but with George's words still a little strained, as they strolled alongside the mill pond. Birds, fish and the wild summer berries caught their eyes, their attention and their palates! As they stopped by one particularly fruitful bush, George asked Pete, "Isn't it a bit too far out to relate all the commandments to our relationship with God?"

"Not at all," responded Pete. "Let me ask you a simple question: 'Do you love Barbara?' George's eyes and mouth popped wide open at the mention of Barbara's name.

"Yes, but how?"

Pete cut his response short and continued.

"That love you have means you wouldn't do anything deliberately to harm her. You wouldn't be violent, or steal, or play around, or make cruel fun of her in public, because your love wouldn't let you. Correct?"

George's head was like a nodding dog, bobbing up and down, swivelling from side to side in agreement with Pete's observations.

"George, you have studied the scriptures. What do you think my Lord meant when he said, 'If you look at a woman with adulterous thoughts in your heart you have committed adultery?'"

George just looked at Pete with mouth wide open, blank faced and immobile.

David piped up with a sarcastic tone in his voice.

"Is the dummy dumb as well now?"

The barbed words and the sing-song tone in the voice seemed to snap George back into the here and now, but he was still angry. He rounded on David with venom in his eyes and voice.

"Look you little smart-ass, I believe in God and what's in the Bible, OK! I want to try and answer Pete's questions truth-fully. Not like you giving an answer that could come from any old rag!"

"Ooh! hoity-toity," responded David with a very conde-scending air in his voice.

Pete stopped walking as the heated exchange took place, as if wanting to distance himself from it.

George and David drew deep breaths as if preparing for the next salvo and, in doing so, realized that Pete was no longer with them. They stopped, looked around and saw Pete some distance back. Embarrassment and regret filled the minds of both men as they looked at each other. Without saying a word, together they walked back to where Pete was standing. Pete stood for a few moments, ignoring the two friends as they approached, quietly looking across the river. He turned to face them.

"There are many hidden secrets between you that cause you both great pain."

George and David looked at each other with faces that expressed shock, guilt and a 'how do you know that truth that has never been spoken of?'

"Hidden prejudices in a person, if left unchecked and unre-solved, will grow, creating divisions and enable the sourness of anger to ferment. They in turn will disable and ultimately cripple the relationship, spoiling its beauty and causing it to fail and die. If, however, you have a trusted friend, the deeper the trust, the more open, the more vulnerable you become to each other. Trust and friendship at any level involves sharing information, history, loves, life concepts, ideas, dislikes and much more. The trust and vulnerability that each gives to the other in the sharing is a beautiful thing and should be cherished, and not used as a weapon by divulging the information to others.

"In a true friendship, the harsh judgement, the black and white of the law and the judgemental approach of others is inappropriate. When presented with a poor situation, gently, with humour tease out the facts, the deeper reasons and hidden pains and reasons for them. Then, and only then, with care and without a personal agenda help the other to 'work through' the situation. You both say you are 'good friends' yet have many disruptive secrets that disable the 'good' in your friendship. Those disruptive secrets prevent trust from developing, cause prejudices to multiply and anger to be commonplace, like now! Be truthful, open, honest, brave and trusting, but most of all loving towards each other. Let that brotherly love, that affection you have for each other, blossom. Like a good gardener, tend your relationship with care, help it to mature, feed and water it so that it can produce beautiful flowers in abundance."

George and David, like naughty school boys, looked at the ground with guilty, uncertain expressions not knowing what to do or say.

Pete turned, looking across the river, and once again became engrossed in something on the opposite bank. Like a shallow, but noisy brook the two began to apologize, but Pete continued to focus intently on the opposite bank, ignoring them. David and George looked at each other, question marks on their faces, not sure what to do or what to say that might turn the clock back and reinstate harmony.

Pete pointed to the opposite bank.

"Can you see those hedge sparrows below the bush over there?"

The question marks on their faces grew deeper, turning their faces into caricatures from a satirical magazine.

"They look happy and content, don't they?"

The two friends had large frowns and now even larger question marks, but they nodded in agreement while the question marks became illuminated above their heads.

"Like so many, that happiness, that contentment is only skin, or should we say feather, deep."

Pete grinned at his own clever remark, which was totally missed by David and George.

"Put a barn full of food in front of them and they will fight over one grain of wheat that is by the barn door."

The two friends looked at each other, neither willing to speak as their illuminated question marks now began flashing like aircraft beacons.

"You two are like the sparrows. You squabble over one or two grains of wheat when a whole barn full of the finest wheat is available to you, if you but asked the right question. If you would listen and learn to love, to understand, to trust each other, things would be much, much better. Untainted love hopes and believes that all things will be all right, no matter what. If you learn to love and understand the other's point of view and not to judge on the flimsiest of hearsay or information, your relationship could become something wonderful."

George's head was down, watching his own foot moving left and right in the grass, without purpose, just embarrassment.

David's ashen, contorted face looked towards George hoping for something, but nothing came. With a very audible groan, David grabbed George in an impulsive hug saying.

"I am sorry for being a real ass. I do love you and I want to be real mates together!"

George just stood statue-like, unmoving. He was not sure what to do or how to react. Pete, with the softest and quietest of voices, said, "It's OK George, you can hug him back. Let David see the love you hide away."

Pete's gentle words of affirmation seemed to flick the on switch and George not only grinned like a cat with a face full of cream but hugged and picked up David, embracing him in a giant bear hug.

"Pete, can I ask you a question too?"

"Yes of course you can David. Ask away."

David, with an impish grin on his face, began.

"When the dummy went dumb, what did you mean by 'committing adultery in your mind being the same as actually committing adultery?'"

George began to frown and splutter, until he saw the teasing grin on David's face and the tolerant, fatherly smile on Pete's face.

"When you fall in love with someone you hope that love will remain the same forever. Positive influences and joint experiences will, through time, mature and deepen the love you share. Negative influences can do the opposite and poison the love, causing it to shrivel and die. These are two extremes and the reality for each couple is somewhere in the middle. The middle line for George and Barbara is different from you and Annette; neither is right, neither is wrong, it is just how a couple functions together."

David looked at Pete with very wide eyes full of surprise,

but eyes with a suspicious mark in them, as though they were questioning Pete's knowledge and intentions. Eyes that say 'you know things that you should not know, but how?'

"Yahweh wants all His children to love their partners with and from an open heart. That love and openness should be for life. The same is true, and even more so, with our love for Yahweh Himself. The unfortunate thing is many other emotions, habits and traits sometimes from childhood play a significant role and imprison or even destroy the love that formed the foundation of their initial relationship. The committing of adultery and any other sin or mistake often depends on the person's state of mind."

"How do you mean?" questioned David. "Surely a sin is a sin whatever your state of mind?"

"That's true," continued Pete. "But it is often the intention in a person's mind that makes an action truly a sin. You see, you can commit a sin by accident, unintentionally, or to protect someone or yourself from harm. These types of sin are often followed almost immediately by regret, pangs of the conscience over what has transpired. To look at another person lustfully, with a suggestion of what you would like to do with them, may come because of the general behaviour on a boys' or girls' night out. In essence, a mistake fed by poor behaviour, drink and so on. To look at a woman and coldly or lustfully plan in your mind, possibly in detail, what you would like to do is altogether a very different way of looking at them. Through the cold calculated planning you have and are committing adultery, all be it in your mind, just as much as if you were holding them physically in your arms. The same is true of a person's love for Yahweh. You can say 'I love Yahweh' but then commit adultery by lusting after money or power fuelled by pride or some other imitation of God."

As they rounded the final bend, the three friends could see the Black Swan but they continued to just amble along as if time was timeless. Progress was being made as they walked, but at a snail's pace. There seemed to be no hurry, as if they all wanted the walk of exploration and understanding to continue. In their minds, the inn seemed to be the point at which their world of discovery was to end.

"I don't think what you have said is kosher, Pete," suggested George.

"Surely a sin is a sin and all require punishment no matter what! The Bible tells us, in some instances, that the sin, and the punishment, due on a father is passed down to his sons' sons. I know God can and does forgive, but we still have to be willing to accept the punishment he gives us."

"That is true to a point George, but there are many shades of grey between black and white."

"Yes but, as I said, a sin is a sin! God doesn't split hairs. If you steal a pen or steal a million pounds it's still stealing in his eyes and you will and should be punished for it. When you read the scriptures there are many instances of people being punished, sometimes harshly, for what we now would consider quite small sins, if a sin at all. So I think you are wrong to split hairs over whether adultery is only in the mind or not. You have committed the sin, so you should be punished for it, no matter what!"

Pete just let out a long thoughtful 'hmmm', while David just looked at the ground with a hangdog expression, like a naughty boy trying to avoid being included in the challenge brought on by George's tone of conversation.

"There is a big difference between the way we look at things and the way Yahweh looks at things. First off, we don't always have all the information. And I don't mean the easy stuff, what we hear or know or read about. But the hidden parts: what has happened over the years, why is a person as they are, what caused the parting of the ways? The people involved may not fully understand themselves, or be able to put it into words, so how are we to know who is right and who is wrong? We often judge without all the information. We also pass sentence and give out punishment, often hurtful and without regard for the other person. We often administer justice harshly on others. That is till it is our turn to be in the dock and then we plead for mercy and understanding.

"Yahweh, on the other hand, knows all that's gone on. Historically, how the relationship formed, how it matured, what caused the cracks to appear, what was done by each person to heal them, the list is endless. But the big difference, and it is huge, is that Yahweh knows the true intentions of the heart. You can lie to me, George, to David, with the utmost sincerity and we wouldn't know because we can't see what is in your mind, let alone what is in your heart! You see our love, regardless of who it is with, is conditional. I know you love Barbara very much, but if she stopped making you those wonderful evening meals would you love her as much? Initially, yes of course you would, but over time the loss could become a hairline crack that would widen when another painful wedge was hammered into it."

"It would help him lose a few pounds around the middle," quipped David.

George said nothing but gave David one of those withering looks that would burn toast at a thousand yards. Pete continued.

"Yahweh is timeless. We, however, have one lifetime on Earth. For Him our lifetime is such a tiny span of time, so why does he care for what we call humankind, let alone any one individual? Because he loves us! Despite all our problems,

Yahweh is still willing to work with each of us as an individual, to draw us together, to help us live together and to draw us to Himself in love and harmony. Yahweh's love is unconditional! He continues to love us and works with us to help us improve, despite our mistakes. He can see our inner potential and His love hopes that one day we will reach that potential and love Him without any restrictions."

David piped up in a sing-song voice.

"But I don't have a relationship with God so why does it matter to me what he thinks or does? What I do is my business and no one else's."

Pete just smiled benignly at David.

"How wrong you are and how far from the truth on all counts!"

Chapter 8

Steak and Ale

The mood of the three friends was thoughtful and lukewarm, to say the very least, as they reached the garden terraced area of the Black Swan but, as in nature, understanding and quiet rebuilding comes after the storm. Sitting down at an empty garden table, they perused the menu discussing what each was going to order. George, following his loud statements of earlier, went for the steak and ale pie with chips and garden peas. David opted for a full blown mixed grill as he remembered, what seemed a lifetime ago, he had reminded George 'it was his shout'! As for Pete, no matter how much the friends tried to cajole him he settled on the fish pie.

"I never could get on with all this meat and blood," he commented. "Even though I have it on the highest authority it's OK to eat. I still find it hard to do so!"

Once again, George and David, looking at each other, had question marks all over their faces, not understanding Pete's comment. Before either could ask the question, the waitress arrived. Sue was plainly but smartly dressed in black slacks and white blouse. She was of medium height and had light auburn hair.

"Good morning gentlemen. Welcome to the Black Swan. I am Sue and your waitress for today. Would you like to order your drinks while looking at the menu? We have several special mains and desserts today, which you will find on the separate sheet."

They all agreed, giving Sue their drinks order. The little group checked the specials on the separate sheet, but could find nothing to tempt their palates. Sue returned from the bar in a very few minutes with their drinks. The trio placed their mains order with Sue, who indicated that it would take about fifteen minutes to arrive. The tables in the garden area were well spaced, each one having a different perspective of the upper mill pond, the river and the flora and fauna that danced in the gentle breeze or played in the branches. Our three travellers chatted aimlessly while admiring their surroundings and observing and acknowledging in a casual, nice way their fellow customers.

David broke the time of peace and quiet with a drawn out, sing-song "Peee-te", like a child wanting something from their parent.

"You have tried to tell us how the commandments relate as much to God as they do to us and about love, but I don't understand how they all fit together? Or how they apply to George and me?"

"That's a fair question," injected George. "Because there is a lot in what you have said I am not sure of or comfortable with!"

Pete just smiled as he looked at both David and George, and nodded in acknowledgement of their request.

"David, have you ever seen the drawings done by the Celtic people?"

"What, you mean the weird looking animals and people they drew around their writings and the impossible patterns they drew, like a ball of string that's been played with by a cat!"

George chortled to himself and mumbled, "Philistine!"

"Something like that," nodded Pete with a smile on his face. He continued, "The patterns have many interpretations. One is they are representations of eternity because there is no beginning and no end to the cord of the pattern. Another is the intertwining of love in our lives. With love, the more parts of our life it touches, the greater the influence it has on the whole of our life."

Pete stopped, as though stunned, seemingly mid-sentence and gazed into the distance, searching the horizon. George and David looked at each other with quizzical looks, not knowing what was happening. Why had Pete stopped? Was he having a fit? Was he in pain or having a heart attack? These and many more were just some of their unspoken questions?

Pete stopped looking and continued as if nothing had happened.

"You know, one of the commandments asks you to honour your father and mother."

They both nodded.

"Another way of interpreting that is to say 'love your father and mother' in a very special way, and in fact, other people too. That special love is from deep inside and is not selfish, but is a love that gives of itself freely, without reserve and without any ulterior reason."

"But doesn't that leave you open to being hurt and abused by other people?" questioned David.

"Yes it does!" was Pete's instant response.

"George, you are a man who has studied the scriptures."

George drew himself up to his full height, attentive, anticipating the question and planning an in-depth theological answer. Pete again stopped and began looking around and into the far distance, eyes not blank but focused so far into the distance that nothing near seemed to register. After a short span of time, Pete again continued as if nothing had happened.

"What do you think brought Simon Peter to tears when he was in the high priest's courtyard?"

George sat upright, chest puffed out with a large intake of breath, ready to speak when David groaned.

"Oh no, not a great theological sermon!"

George ignored him and began, "There are many possible reasons. Some say it was Simon Peter's lack of courage."

Pete's head shook gently side to side and hung down.

"Others say it was because he had let Jesus down, others that he had not listened to the warning that Jesus had given him and was embarrassed because of it. Still others that he was frightened because of where he was and did not dare say he was one of Jesus' followers."

Pete's head hung even lower when a pleasant, concerned voice said, "Is your friend all right?"

Pete's head popped up like a ball in a bath and looked straight at the smiling face of Sue.

"Yes! I am fine. Just a little dispirited, but fine."

She smiled back and asked, "Whose is the steak and ale pie?"

George's hand shot up as if it was attached to a Saturn Five rocket.

"That's mine," was his response.

"And the mixed grill?" David signalled in a more genteel manner.

"And the fish pie would be yours, sir! Do enjoy your meal."

They all responded with 'thank you' and then began to tuck into the steaming food. It is often said 'silence comes with good food' and this meal was no exception.

As they ate, Pete's times of looking around seemed to increase and he was to George and David's eyes becoming more and more agitated. Pete continued looking between mouthfuls of his fish pie. "It is a pity that no one can look into those eyes and see what I saw. The world looks only on the negative in me, the response of a weak man watching his best friend being condemned to death."

The two friends looked at each other with blank faces. They could see Pete's physical distress and hear the emotional distress in his voice, but did not understand why? Most of all, George took on a matter of fact, almost condescending air.

"Well what do you expect? Peter did not listen to Jesus and, being hotheaded, he put himself in harm's way."

"All that is true. But that unselfish love, it poured out from those eyes in such waves I never thought possible. It was the realization of just how much love there was for me and what that love was willing to do, to bear, for me. It was too much to bear. Even with all my weaknesses, my darkest moment, his love for me, for all of us, was shining brighter than the midday sun."

"And that love is still there as bright for you today!"

Pete spun round, head, shoulders, his whole body, to see a middle-aged man dressed in slacks and T-shirt.

"My Lord!" was all that Pete could say as he launched himself at Jay, embracing him in a rib-crushing bear hug.

After a short interlude, Pete unwrapped himself and introduced Jay to George and Pete. George took on the role of host, busying himself ordering new drinks for all.

He turned to David and rather pompously said to Sue, "Put everything on one bill and David will settle up at the end." At the same time, he stuck out a finger like an accusing arrow and pointed at him.

David was caught off guard, not expecting to have to pay for all four, but meekly nodded with a thin smile of agreement and acknowledgement to Sue.

Taking a sip from his wine, Jay looked at the three friends and asked what they had been discussing? George again took the lead, saying, "We were discussing St Peter at the trial and all his mistakes."

"That's not the whole picture," snorted David. "We had started talking about the commandments and how they relate to both us and God and then we went on to talk about love and how that influences our lives."

"My! My! That's a huge set of topics. Have you come to any conclusions?" asked Jay.

"Not really," replied David. "In some ways I am more confused, but in others I understand a little more."

George giggled to himself.

"It does not take much to confuse you and, as to understanding, if you can't add or subtract it you're lost…"

Jay stopped George in mid-sentence.

"That is a little unkind George. David's point of view is just as valid as yours, as are anyone's, especially if they are from deep within their heart."

Jay sat quietly just playing with his glass of wine, swilling the liquid around and breathing in its bouquet.

"George, in simple terms, what do you think Yahweh considers as the most important thing between you and Him?"

George's face went white as the colour drained away and a blank expression descended.

"I have no idea," was the mute response.

Jay smiled warmly.

"It's OK, it is not a theology exam. Don't forget, Jesus had to teach Galilean fishermen first."

Pete coughed into his glass, while Jay just smiled gently.

"Yahweh's greatest concern is your relationship with Him.

He loves you and all He wants is for you to love Him in return. His love for you is the very best of a father's to a child, a husband's to a wife, a brother's to a sister, a friend to a friend, all these and many more wrapped up in one love. Yahweh's love comes directly from His heart, it is a gift without limits. It is a pure love that will go to any length to encourage, to forgive, to guide and help a person to love Him in return. He will even accept you saying 'no' and having no relationship with Him at all!"

Jay looked longingly at David, who met Jay's steady, loving gaze for a microsecond before looking away.

"But His love is so great it will let you go without condemnation or bitterness, but He will still continue to care for you and encourage you in the hope that one day you may love Him in return."

"If it is that simple, why do we get it so wrong? What's the purpose of the law and why all the punishment we read about in the Bible?" questioned George.

"Loving Yahweh and His gift of grace is just that simple George!"

"Oh!" stuttered George.

"But humankind does find it hard to have a relationship with Yahweh. Its very nature towards Him changed at what you call 'the fall' and that brought many problems. The hard part now, for humankind, comes in two parts: to love Yahweh with a pure love that emanates from deep within each heart. Secondly, to overcome the many self-centred desires of human nature."

Jay paused, taking a sip of wine, smiling warmly at the little group as he did so.

"If your love is 'skin deep' it fails quickly because it has no depth. Like seed in shallow soil, it has no depth, no strong root system to draw on the deep store of water below when a drought or testing times come. It is the same with your love. If this has no depth, no reserves of love to call upon, it will not have the resilience to survive and flourish."

Looking deeply into the eyes of George, he continued.

"You love Barbara don't you?"

George sat bolt upright, initially with a shocked look on his face at Jay's words. As Jay continued, George's expression became curious, but with a hint of guarded suspicion.

"Your love is very deep for her, but it is not entirely self-giving."

George spluttered, trying to make up a sentence but without success. David, on the other hand, remained deathly quiet and seemed to shrink under the table as though not wishing to be a part of this conversation or any one like it.

"There are parts of your love for Barbara that are made up of a mixture of real love and love that comes from your wants and desires, especially when you want and get your own way so you can play bridge two nights a week!"

"How?" questioned George in a high-pitched squeak as his jaw hit the floor and his face turned bright pink. Composing himself. "That's not fair Jay, we both have things we do by mutual agreement, like this weekend and Barbara's school reunion."

"That is very true George and you do have many things you do, as you put it, 'by mutual agreement'. Look deeper into your heart at some of the things you do that are to your personal gain and which Barbara has had to give up something of hers to let you have your way. That is the selfish self-centred part of human nature that colours part of the love you have to offer as it does many others."

George's face was now criss-crossed with deep lines

that contorted his now florid face. Jay reached out and took a reluctant hand, holding it firmly but in a strange way with great gentleness and love. Time passed, but in a blink of an eye George's face drained of all its upset and pain. His face took on a gentle serene look of realization. He looked firstly at Pete, whose smiling face seemed to be surrounded by a glow that was hard to describe or pin down. Then at David, who was still trying to hide his frightened 'don't ask me any questions about this subject' face under the table. Finally, if reluctantly, George looked into the eyes of Jay. His eyes locked like a spigot in its hole, a hand in its glove, with those deep pools, pouring out love, facing him.

"Yahweh's love for you has no selfishness; it is a pure love deep from within His heart. He wants your love for Him, for Barbara, David, for everyone else, to be the same, pure without any selfish desires. Most of all, He wants that love to come from deep within a heart that is totally in love with Him."

George's face became strained again as he spoke. "I thought I was! I thought I knew how, but I am not sure any more!"

His head dropped as if a master switch had been thrown. David's trembling hand reached out and touched George's arm.

"It's OK mate, God will forgive you because he knows you love Him and He loves you."

"How true your words are shrimp!" said Jay smiling: a little twinkle in his eye. "The words you have spoken, given to you by Yahweh, are meant for you as much as for George!"

David's face was one of shock and confusion at Jay's response as he mulled the words over in his mind. Pete just grinned at him like the proverbial Cheshire cat.

"Welcome to the 'Simon Peter' club David!"

David just looked at Pete in total bewilderment.

"You have been inspired by Yahweh; you speak of His love and show His compassion for George from deep within your own heart! What a joy to know that, given the right prompt, you are willing to release your true love from the cage you keep it in and let it see the light of day!"

"Oh!" was David's stunned, simple response.

Chapter 9

To the Bar and Back

Their conversations continued back and forth as waves crash on to a beach and, once spent, ebb back under the next wave. The main course, too, had been long spent, as had the drinks. Jay offered to order whatever desserts people wanted and the next round of drinks. With an appropriate wave of the hand and short conversation, Sue duly gave the group the dessert menu.

Menus deliberated over, two lists were compiled ready for Jay to deliver to Sue, who was thought to be in the bar. David offered to go with Jay, saying in an impish way, "I'll help you carry the drinks back and make sure you don't get lost."

Jay smiled and nodded in agreement. The two disappeared quickly into the inn's rear bar entrance, finding their way down an old narrow corridor into the main bar. The room was of a reasonable size with a single row of tables around the outer wall. Other guests were seated around the tables on a combination of chairs and wall-mounted high-backed bench seats. The room however, was dominated by the majestic three-sided bar. The bar's dark wood glowed with the polish and love of the many publicans who had served and cared for the inn over the years. The ornate canopy above the bar hid, from the front at least, a variety of hanging stemmed glasses. Below these, on large wooden pegs, hung the pint and half pint glass tankards and to one side a smaller number of pewter tankards; these being the personal drinking vessels of the inn's regular patrons.

Jay gave the food and drink order to the barman. Before preparing the drinks, he passed the dessert order to Sue, who had served them in the garden and was busy preparing another table's order.

Speaking to David, she said, "I'll bring the desserts out to your table when they are ready."

He nodded his agreement. As they waited for the drinks to be poured, Jay asked David if he came here often.

"No!" was the reply, "I prefer the Greyhound over in Churnton."

"Why is that?" asked Jay.

"I have more friends over that way; only George here-a-bouts."

"Is it true to say 'friends' or would it be more truthful to say 'a special friend' in Churnton?"

David's eyes narrowed into slits and, like an animal being backed into a corner, his muscles tensed as if ready to execute a defensive strike.

With a little more force in his voice than was needed, David answered, "I am not sure what you mean, I have many friends over in Churnton!"

"Again that is true, but Simone is a special friend isn't she?"

Like the jaw of a cartoon character, David's went straight to the floor and an expression of bewilderment and panic strained every muscle in his face.

"Do you love Simone?"

The panic in David's face deepened as he looked around the bar, expecting all the other guests to have heard Jay's question. What and how was he to respond to this man? If they were listening would gossip then go round the villages and back to Anne? Panic on panic flooded David's mind as thoughts, scenarios, implications and actions whirled around. Jay smiled a very gentle reassuring and loving smile.

"It's OK, they are not listening to us. Their minds are full of their own thoughts and needs."

David gazed into Jay's eyes, which seemed to have a limitless and timeless depth. Reassurance and a strange sensation of love seemed to flow from those eyes, calming his panic inside and much more.

"Yes, I do love her," was the almost inaudible, strained whispered reply.

"But you are married to Anne aren't you?" was Jay's response.

"I am!" David said with some bitterness.

"But our relationship has died. We live more as brother and sister now. There is, and has been for some time, little enjoyment between us and I am finding it hard to…"

"What happened to the marriage vows you took all those years ago. Did you not believe in them when you said them?" interrupted Jay.

"Yes I did!" was the swingeing response. "I know I have made many many mistakes in my life, but I have tried to remain faithful, to do my duty to love and look after Anne."

"But did not those vows say 'for better or for worse'?"

"That's a smart alec question, you know full well that they do."

"So why have you given up when you are in the middle of the worst bit?"

David's face began to flush into a deep crimson and knot angrily as though someone was twisting it like wringing out water from a wet towel.

"I tried to be a good husband, but the more I tried the more my needs seemed to be ignored and the more demands were being put on my time, often for silly things."

"So your love began to die for selfish reasons then!" stated Jay.

"Depending on your point of view, I suppose you could be right. But why should I be the one that has had to give up so much," wailed David.

"Do you not think that Anne will have given up many things herself?"

"I suppose so!"

"Do you not think it is worth another try to see if you can rekindle the love you once had?"

"No!" came from David's lips with a cry of panic as tears began to flow down his now florid face. "It has been too long and we have had too many tries that have come to nothing. My heart does not believe that if Anne said 'she would try again' that it would come to anything. For the first few weeks, months and maybe years we would be OK, but I would be frightened that, in time, we would be back as we are now. Time lost and maybe the love I have found, and Simone herself, lost!"

"Could Anne not say the same of you?" challenged Jay.

David dejectedly nodded his head in agreement, but said nothing.

"Are you comfortable with that?"

"With what?"

Came David's sharp reply.

"With a failed or failing marriage, no faith in your wife and an adulterous relationship with Simone?"

"No of course I am not happy with it, but what am I supposed to do? Do I stay with Anne and be unhappy? And live without the laughter and joy that Simone gives me?"

"You could tell Anne the truth and seek a divorce."

"I suppose you are right, but she will take me to the cleaners."

"So which do you want; your house, money and gadgets you have now, without happiness, or a life of limited comforts but happy?"

David thought for a very few seconds before saying in a firm deliberate voice, "Happiness!"

Jay smiled at David.

"That's a good choice because with true happiness you can do without many of the things humankind holds important and overcome almost anything, especially when you have someone to share the happiness with!"

"Do you approve of divorce then?" queried David.

"That is a no win type of question. The ideal, the way my Father wanted it, is to have a relationship that lasts a lifetime, but humankind is fickle, mistakes are made and emotions get turned around. Once turned around, the laws of love and forgiveness are forgotten and the laws of retribution and greed that humankind has developed are used to their full force."

"By 'Father' do you mean God?"

"Yes!" came the simple reply.

"So God is OK with divorce?"

Jay smiled a Cheshire cat type grin before continuing, "I have had many other leading questions that have been set up to trap me, but I led myself into that one!"

David just frowned.

"How come you call God 'Father?' Do you know Him? Do you love Him intimately as if He was your father?"

Jay smiled one of those smiles from inside a person that radiates to all points of the compass bringing warmth, certainty, surety and a knowing from deep inside.

"'Yes' is the simple answer on all counts and many more!"

"Does God, your Father love a person like me?"

"Yes, without a doubt!"

"Oh!"

"My Father loves all His children and has always wanted us to be happy together. Sadly, others wanted to upset the harmony we all had and played on humankind's weaknesses. That led to what you call 'The Fall', but our Father still loves His children and is forgiving and tolerant of the many things they do wrong. My Father's loving tolerance, some call grace, others foolishness and still others rely on the law and its punishments. Think of your namesake, a man after my Father's heart who committed murder and adultery. He said he was sorry from the deepest reaches of his heart and My Father forgave him. Not only did He forgive him but gave him a son in Solomon that any father would be proud of."

"Oh, King David!" mumbled David.

Jay smiled before continuing.

"The Hebrew nation and its kings committed adultery over many years…"

David's hand went up!

"What do you mean 'the kings and nation committed adultery'?"

"They worshipped other gods and those given special roles used them to their own ends, to rob those who came to worship My Father."

"That's not very nice, why would they do that?"

"The reasons they or anyone would do that can be one word or a list as long as your arm! The letter 'P' covers five that will give you an idea: Power, Pride, Position, Popularity and Possessions."

"What's wrong with those? They are commonplace and in many places are applauded by many people."

"That is very true but they, in different ways, lock away the beauty of an open loving heart. People may do many good things. But are they done out of kindness or for what they get in return? None of them are done for the beauty of love! Thankfully, there are those who do try from within their heart to do what my Father would have them do. They are often downtrodden or restricted in some way by those with other motives. The beauty is that my Father's love shines through no matter what, nothing can stop it. An open 'Father-centred heart' is a brother or sister to me and is a joy to all who need comfort, love and reassurance."

"So what should I do now?"

"That question, in truth, only you can answer," responded Jay.

"But can you not tell me or guide me in the right direction?"

"No! There is no right or wrong direction that anyone can give you. Yes there is the ideal, a loving marriage for a lifetime and that is what my Father would wish. But, because of the tainted cocktail of human emotions, that cannot always be maintained. In any relationship you mix two unique sets of emotions that may, with work, last a lifetime, but could just as easily, even with work, fail."

"Oh! So the decision to leave or stay with Anne is down to me."

"Correct! Master Jedi."

David looked at Jay with a pained and bemused look on his face. How come this man seemed to know so much about himself? Why was he able to help in so many ways; to speak the truth without being hurtful and to guide without being directive?

"Jay?" questioned David. "When I asked you about your relationship with God, who you call Father, and whether you knew Him? You said 'yes'! The way you talk you make it sound as though you really have an intimate relationship with Him! As if you actually were His son?"

"I am!" came Jay's simple response.

David recoiled at the simplicity, yet profoundness, of Jay's words.

"But I thought Jesus was God's only son!"

In a gentle, yet strangely powerful, voice Jay said, "I am Jesus!"

David's face became a kaleidoscope of expressions as Jay's words filled his mind and heart. Realization and possibilities began to slowly filter in as his voice exclaimed, "Jesus!"

The barman broke the turmoil in David's mind.

"There are your drinks gentlemen. Would you like them putting on your tab?"

"Yes please," responded Jay with a smile.

The barman nodded in acknowledgement, saying, "The waitress will bring your desserts out to the garden in a little while."

"Come on David, let's take these out to the other two before they die of thirst!"

David's pained expression of wonderment began to fade and be replaced with a watery smile.

The two chatted as close friends as they passed through the narrow passageway and out into the brightness of the afternoon sun, ambling up to George and Pete. George's face changed as he saw the two approaching, but recovered a sense of composure as they placed the drinks on the table.

Pete asked the question, "What's happened to the desserts?"

David responded in a happy, chatty way, "The waitress is bringing them out as soon as they are ready."

Jay nodded in agreement. Moments later, Sue appeared with a tray loaded down with the four desserts.

As she began to hand them around, asking whose was which, George, in a less than kind and demanding voice, said, "Mine is the blackberry and apple pie."

As he said it, he reached across the table, almost grabbing the pie from her hand. An unnatural silence fell across the table.

Her words, "Do enjoy your desserts," broke the silence.

The pies, gateaux and ice cream were devoured with great enjoyment and light-hearted conversation flew back and forth across the table.

Chapter 10

Walk with ME

The little group sat for a while chatting about nothing in general: just chatting. George, however, kept prodding David for information, trying to find out what had gone on in the bar. David's red, tear-stained face was the magnet that George could not resist; he just had to know what had happened. David and the others, however, just ignored George's comments and kept on talking about the world and life in general, which only made George more frustrated. His desire to know what had happened, in all the gory details, the 'whys' and 'wherefores' was being thwarted. What Jay had said earlier burned like an inferno in his mind.

Pete and David began talking quietly about personal joint experiences and the implication of Jay's words in their old lives, and the possibilities in David's life to come. George was looking at Jay with a blank, embarrassed expression as though not sure what to say or how to begin a conversation. A gentle, loving smile began to flow across Jay's face, touching every part as it did so.

"George, come walk with me!" were the words spoken by Jay that lay somewhere between an invitation and a command.

George got up without argument, responding with the word, "OK!"

Jay placed his hand on Pete's shoulder, saying, "Be back in a little while."

Pete acknowledged the words with a small nod and a generous smile.

Walking through the inn's garden, Jay looked at George and asked, "Why are you jealous of David and why do you think I should have spoken to you first?"

George's jaw just fell open, and then moved up and down mumbling reasons and excuses that had no real meaning at all.

"You are a man who has studied the scriptures so that you can teach others."

George nodded; his eyes wide open in surprise but with a hint of trepidation on his face at what was to follow.

"What do you think was meant by the story of me washing the disciples' feet?"

As the question penetrated his mind, George's face raced from panic to 'I know that answer' followed by a little pigeon chest as he said, "To be a good kind leader and to be humble and a servant of all!"

"That's a fair answer, so why don't you do what you have said?"

George's face went paler than the whitest of snow and even his open gaping, fish-like mouth took on the pallor of pale grey.

"The leadership part is easy: man trains you for that as that is where men want to be; the head over others, the leader. What my training teaches you is how to be at the bottom of man's pile, yet at the top. Many children aspire to riches, accolades, titles and all sorts of other gifts for their own glory, whereas I ask you to give the glory to Yahweh in thanks for the gifts he has given you."

Jay looked at George and asked, "Do you understand?"

"Not really," came the downhearted response.

"You call me 'the servant king', and rightly so. Many call themselves 'my servants' and at face value that too is right.

The sad part is, like yourself, the idea of being a servant is only at the surface. It does not penetrate to the heart. The idea of leadership, power and privilege, however, entices and entangles and reaches the heart of everyone and puffs up their idea of personal self-importance. You feel you have no need of help and yet, because of your idea of position, you felt it was you I should have spoken to first!"

If George's face could have got any paler it would have done so as it hung seemingly by a thread to his shoulders. His eyes, still wide open, now had a watery film over them.

"I don't understand," was George's pitiful cry.

Jay continued, "I love Yahweh and came to serve Him and humankind. If you truly open your heart you will see beyond the expectations, requirements and desires of man. My hope, my desire, for you, is that you too will love Yahweh with an open, unrestricted heart. And with your heart filled with His love you can serve others in His name and mine.

"David is in turmoil, crying inside, and is in desperate need. He needs your love, help and understanding: not condemnation using unfounded judgments based on man's interpretation of the law. Yahweh loves all His children, His gift of 'grace' was poured out through me, satisfying all the requirements of the law fully!

"In your own way, George, you too need love and help if you would but allow me into your heart. I can and am willing to speak up for you and to do all in my power to help you. But you have got to say 'yes' from your heart and let me help you to change your priorities inside, and help you to truly come closer to me."

George looked up and, with a great wail that came from deep inside, said, "But I gave myself to Jesus and his Church a long time ago and they said I was called by him to be a teacher, a leader!"

Jay gently rested his hand on George's shoulder, "All that you have said is true, but like so many it is still only at the surface. The seed that was planted has not been allowed to put its roots into your heart. The seed that was sown within you is surrounded by the briars of the world, which choke the goodness from the seed and prevent its roots reaching into your heart."

"If that is the case, how do I go deeper? How do I open my heart? How do…"

Jay held up his hand, stopping a potentially never ending list from George.

"George, you know of me and understand much of what is in the scriptures, but you do not know me, intimately! Look at the river. That is you. It is bubbling full of ideas, knowledge gained, things to say, people to help. But, like you, the river is shallow and even the small rocks on the river bed disturb and move the water about from one place to another, as do the rocks in your life. Take David's problem. You hear things, understand a little of what is going on. YOU make judgments and decide what is right and what is the best way forward for him without knowing the whole story."

"But he is committing adultery!" screeched George.

"That is true," said Jay. "But so are you!"

George's face became bright red. His body tensed, taking on a fierce aggressive stance. His voice became sharp and curt. "I am NOT committing adultery and never have!"

Jay looked at him with a soulful expression, gently shaking his head, "Against Barbara what you say is true, but against Yahweh and me you have and do commit adultery!"

"What do you mean against you, I hardly know you so how can I commit adultery against you. We are not in a relationship!"

"That is sadly very true! You say you hardly know me! That

is the foundation of the problem, that you do not know me or have a relationship with me, but you do many things in my name! Many of the things you do are in 'man's' strength and ways, but not mine!"

Jay paused and a deep silence covered the two. Even the river seemed to go quiet, stilling its waters, as if waiting for a profound word or touch of love from Jay.

"Adultery, in its simplest form, is the act of not keeping a promise. You have broken your promise by seeking out something or an accolade from someone that you value more than Yahweh. You often make promises to me like, 'I will pray for the people on my list every day or I will go to the midweek service, but go to the cinema instead!' Is the cinema more important than being with and in the presence of God? Think of the Scriptures, how often they refer to the Hebrew nation committing adultery towards Yahweh. At the time, they were praying to other gods or using the gifts of God for their own ends and glorification, like the Temple and the Laws given through Moses."

For some time, George's head had hung down, chin on chest. As he thought about what Jay had said, it seemed to get even lower.

"George?" questioned Jay. "Do you see those beautiful white swans upstream in the river's deeper water?"

He looked and nodded.

"They are regal, heads held high with a plumage of the purest white. But if you look closer you can see their contrasting areas of black, grey and orange. They are not all pristine white, or pure and innocent in temperament, but like yourself they are flawed and, like the nickname you give this pub, are Mucky Ducks!"

"Jay, are you saying that much of what I do is wrong in God's eyes?"

"No! You are just misguided, led astray by humankind and its ways that flatter self. Humankind has many wants and needs, for power, pride, popularity and possessions, wealth, position and authority over others. Pride is the most damaging because it provides excuses, acceptable reasons for all the others."

George frowned, not fully understanding the implications of what Jay had said, but remained silent trying to collect his own thoughts.

"Look back to the river George from the place where we are standing. To our right is the shallow turbulent water, in front is the transition as the turbulent water enters the pool and to our left is the deep, apparently slow moving, pool. Many think they know me when they are in the turbulent shallow waters becoming excited by the turbulence, not realizing it is the stones in the river bed that change the water's direction, not me. In the same way, humankind's desires act like stones in your life and change the direction and how you interact with others and Yahweh. Even small stones can change and cause great damage to your relationship with Yahweh when your spiritual water is shallow.

"But as the river's water and your spiritual water deepens from turbulent shallows to the deep pool, the stones of life have less influence on the water's direction and flow. Yes, the stones may still cause some turbulence on the surface, but their effect is far less. For those who want to and are willing to step out into the even deeper water and become part of me, and me part of them, the effect of the world's largest stones is minimized. The relationship I hope for with you becomes much deeper and more intimate. I will support and care for you, and for all who trust and believe in me."

George looked at the river with a bemused face, trying to understand and fully comprehend the meaning and importance of Jay's words.

"You said earlier you had been called to be a teacher, a leader. And so you have, but not in the way you have interpreted those words."

George looked at Jay with questions, sadness and confusion written all across his face, while his mouth formed unspoken words.

"Yahweh's call was a request to serve Him and His children. Sadly, humankind places its own rules and interpretation on Yahweh's call, expecting everyone to conform to one tradition or another. Each tradition moulds a person's call, expecting them to conform to the ways and ideologies that have been built up over many years. Those that are different are often shunned. Those too that have a real desire to be led by My Father and try to do things His way are often vilified or ridiculed by many."

George's face was blank, expressionless, hearing Jay's words, but not understanding what he was saying or the true impact of their meaning.

"The call you were given was a request from Yahweh to follow Him in my footsteps. Humankind is wrapped up in the five 'P's' and interprets all physical things and many spiritual things based on them. Yahweh has no interest in the physical things of humankind. Yahweh's interest is in having a loving relation with you, and all humankind, that grows in and from the individual's heart.

"Yahweh was, and still is, asking you to guide His children as I did. Gently, yet firmly, with words of direction, but with a loving touch, with actions of strength, but with the caress of a butterfly's wing. To lead not with orders, rules or driving a person onwards as a modern shepherd would, but as a shepherd who guides from within the heart of the flock; a fellow traveller, guiding, pointing the way, encouraging by word and deed and being encouraged. Rejoicing, too, in a fellow traveller who helps you stand upright and apologize when you fall, make a mistake or thoughtlessly speak words that hurt others."

George's eyes and mouth were wide open as the enormity of what Jay was saying began to coalesce and find fertile soil in his mind.

"There are many children Yahweh would like you to touch, to show them their mistaken thoughts and ideals. In the village you have two families that have found spiritual strength in the values of humankind. They are in need of your help and guidance. You will know them by the slogans they have on their cars. They proclaim their belief. Both need your help!

"'One Life. Live it', and 'Love life. Live It'.

"Both slogans are statements of intent and have a certain validity, both contain a truth, but both have a touch of personal selfishness and hopelessness. The second phrase, common to both slogans, 'Live it', obviously refers to life. Linked to the first part of the two phrases, they take on a tone of possessiveness and selfishness. To live your life in whatever you consider the most enjoyable way and to the maximum, regardless of its impact on others. To 'Love life' suggests a person who is inward looking and in love with their way of life and its excesses with little regard for others. To live a life to the maximum is far better than bemoaning life's trials and tribulations, but with consideration and a willingness to help others. The slogan 'One Life. Live it' is a sad expression. I have to say they are mistaken! It suggests to me a person who has little or no hope in their heart for the future! The slogan, sadly, looks only at the lifespan of the earthly body. Yahweh's gift of life is available for all who believe and reach out to Him in their hearts. As you go deeper George, I hope you will help those families: walk alongside them, guide them, pointing the way as

Yahweh's modern day shepherd."

George continued to look at the river as it played over the stones in front of him.

"How can I help people like that? How do I get into the deeper water?"

Jay grinned from ear to ear, "Just trust and jump in."

George frowned, "But how? How do I know it is safe?"

"You don't, that's where faith comes in. You have to want to do it, to believe, to trust that our loving Father's arms are there ready to catch you. And they are!"

George stood frozen like a statue not sure of what to do.

"To say sorry from the heart is a good place to start," said Jay in the most gentlest of voices.

George's stance did not change. His lips moved, but no words came out. Seemingly without warning, his knees buckled and hit the grassy bank. A wail like an old siren came out of his mouth and tears flooded from his eyes with greater force than any circus clown. As George's knees touched the grass, Jay's steadying hand was on his shoulder. Time stood still, yet time passed as the two talked as only two people in love can do. Realization of Jay's true nature filtered into George's heart. Hugs, tears, laughter, words of grace, nods of understanding and many other intimate exchanges took place as the buds of the flowers of love began to swell and burst into full bloom.

As they began their journey back to Pete and David, Jay began to hum a tune.

"Jay, what's the tune you are humming," queried George.

"It's a modern song, called 'On the Edge', that fits the moment and would be a good one for you to listen to. It speaks of a person like you, 'on the edge', challenged by the next step. Like that person, you will agonize over the taking of the next step. But, if you take that step your life will change…"

"My Lord, what is to follow? What happens next?" questioned George.

"Be encouraged in your heart by me! Do not fear the step, the future journey, as I will be with you when you take that first step and many others like it!

"It is a long journey filled with many stones, many briars, but a journey nevertheless with me always near. The deeper the water, the deeper more intimate the relationship. The deeper you are willing to go into, the nearer you come to me. If you hold me at arm's length I can come no closer. Those who try to control me by fixing boundaries and imposing rules on my children, will fight against you and make life painful for you. Remember in your heart our time together for it is our time and, no matter what happens to you, you have known and felt my love and there is nothing humankind can do to change or destroy that. As you continue on your journey with me, listen to My Spirit. He will guide and give counsel."

George's eyes began to fill once again, "You would do that for me?" he questioned.

"We would do that for any of our children no matter what! My Father's love for each child does not change. He will encourage the furthest from Him and the nearest to Him. Those who want to abandon the rigours of the world and be near Him, heart to heart, are very special to Him."

"Can I be like that, heart to heart?" questioned George.

"Anyone can be! All can be if they so wish! Just love Our Father with all your heart and mind, with everything you have. Hold nothing back!"

George just stood there unmoving, trying to understand, to grasp the enormity of what had been said.

"But how?"

"Just love Our Father as intimately as you would and have

loved Barbara," said Jay gently with a radiant smile on his face.

"Come on George! It's time to go back to the others," he added, with an oversized grin on his face.

"Can't we stay for a little longer?" came the heart's crying response.

"No!" said Jay. "We have a relationship to heal, judgemental attitudes and prejudice to remove, understanding and tolerance to impart and the rose of love to nurture."

"That sounds like a lot of work, a lot of things to do. Can I help?" queried George.

"Yes!" was Jay's quick response. "There might just be some things you could help with."

George smiled, puffed up his chest, "OK, let's go then!"

Chapter 11

Pick and Mix!

Jay and George ambled back to the garden with its throng of people all seemingly busy with their own discussions and enjoyments. As they sat down at their table, Jay popped a hand in his pocket, pulled out a note and passed it to Pete. He asked if he would nip to the bar and get another round of drinks. Pete nodded, confirmed everyone's order and set off for the bar. George's face was one of those that could not hide a secret and now was no exception. Eyes dancing and sparkling with laughing, turned up corners, mouth quivering just waiting for the question it wanted so much to answer and a body that seemed to be covered with goose pimples as it gyrated around on the bench seat. David had a face full of curiosity. He could see something was different with George, but did not know what it was or what question to ask, so both sat in frustrated silence. Before David could find the right question to begin the question and answer session George so longed for, Pete arrived back with a tray full of drinks and packets of nibbles, "to keep starvation away," as he put it.

"George, how many commandments do you think David has broken?" questioned Jay.

George's face drained and the exhilarated look vanished. George looked at Jay deflated, like a bouncy castle that had lost its air, his shoulders folded and sank. He looked at David with a pained look that said, 'I do not really want to answer that question'. David's face was a picture of shock, concern and question; what was his friend going to say? George looked to Pete for help and then back to Jay, seeing faces with grins bordering on those of clowns.

"What do you think is so funny?" was his terse question.

"For the moment you have got the wrong David! But ultimately it is a question you need to ask yourself and consider what you do with the answer. Try King David!" was Jay's gentle and compassionate reply.

George rose centimetres in height as the burden was seemingly taken from his shoulders. David gulped his drink trying to settle his over-stretched nerves. George nervously responded, "I guess most of them."

"Hmm!" was Jay's response. "OK! I'll ask the question in reverse. Which ones did he not break?" George hung his head and just shook it in a defeated and dejected fashion. All his hopes, all his anticipation, all his jubilation as he returned to the table was gone in an instant.

"I suppose through his life he must have broken pretty much all of them. He certainly committed adultery, stole from the temple, abused his position, committed murder by proxy and wanted things that were not his to have. I dare say he was not faithful to Yahweh as well."

"That's a fair list," responded Jay. "What was my Father's response towards David's actions?"

"Didn't God kill his child and give David much trouble from his son in later years?"

"Put simply, you are right, but that is not all."

David's glass hit the table with a thump. The other three looked at him in surprise. David spoke tight-lipped but with the force of hurricane in his voice.

"I knew it! God is heartless and unforgiving, even towards

one of His favourite people, so what's the point of even trying to be good and keep the commandments? If you break any of them you are damned for the rest of your life by God and man!"

Jay looked at David with understanding and sadness in his eyes, yet eyes that were full of love. Pete, too, looked at David with concern and with a gentle caress in his voice.

"Take it from one who knows David; you are so far from the real truth as you can be."

"What do you mean, 'knows David'? You weren't there, so how are you going to know the real truth?" was David's bitter reply.

"What you say is true, but I have been in similar situations and I know Yahweh loves us no matter what. Yes, He disciplines us as much as any loving father would, but in doing so helps us to learn, to grow and become better children."

David snorted, "See, you agree!"

Jay remained quiet, knowing David's heart and mind had become fixed. Pete looked across the table at a face contorted by an inner pain, frustration and anger.

"David?" questioned Pete, "Do you remember what Jay said about Peter in the High Priest's home?"

"Sort of."

"What he didn't say was Jesus had warned Peter that Satan was going to try and find a weakness in him and exploit it. The burden of that mistake, of not listening or understanding, led to his downfall and my greatest sadness. That mistake, even though Jesus forgave me, others forced me to carry for the rest of my life. To my sadness, many used it to point fun, to ridicule, others to condemn. And there are still others who use it to undermine my work and the work of others. That mistake, that 'sin', above all that is known about me, showed me to be as fallible and as much a Mucky Duck as you, George or anyone else.

David's head snapped round, his eyes wide open at the strange use of the pub's colloquial name.

"In love, I had no defence; I had done what they said I had done. Jesus forgave me and, as he had said from the cross to all of us, 'It is finished.' It is done with and most of all forgiven and forgotten about, remembered no more! All things finished, completed, in Him and through Him. Having forgiven me, he entrusted me with one of the greatest jobs ever."

Jay's hand gently rested on Pete's arm, his fingers moved slowly back and forth as though lovingly stroking a cat. A troubled tinderbox of silence descended, waiting for the next wrong word that would cause David to ignite and explode.

"David!" said Jay. "You were talking earlier, with Pete and George, about water and how the waves on deep water have little effect on the river bottom."

David frowned, a frown that said 'you weren't there so how do you know?', but nodded in agreement.

"If you love someone and that love is deep within you, you will forgive all manner of upsets and hurts because your love is so strong. What you may do is say, 'I do not like what you have done because it hurts me, but…' If your love is reciprocated, a genuine heartfelt apology will be made from the love the other person has deep within them."

David gave a curt nod of agreement, his eyes dark, sharp and untrusting, ready to attack or defend as the need arose.

"A shallow love, however, may be influenced by power and personal desires or needs, seeking to take from you or stop you doing or enjoying something as a form of punishment. Shallow love that is tainted can also be possessive, jealous, wanting to take the joy of achievement from the other instead of glorying, rejoicing in their achievement.

"The commandments, the law, is a statement of requirements. The first law requires you to 'Love Yahweh with all your heart', others to not act in a way that causes hurt to others; 'not to steal or murder...' The law and its requirements are black and white, as are its punishments. The law has no need of love or compassion as it seeks to point out the error. A law that has been broken requires recompense to the injured party, passes judgment on the law breaker and requires punishment to be carried out. Loving discipline, however, seeks to teach, to encourage a person to be and do better. When my Father disciplines he is seeking to teach, to encourage, and, if the person says sorry from the heart, my Father will love them even more and give them gifts greater than before."

The two friends sat in silence trying to understand and grasp the meaning of Jay's words. Pete sat with a benign smile on his face listening to Jay's words as he looked at other guests in the garden.

"Do you know the story of Job?" questioned Jay.

David's knotted, gnarled, log-like face seemed to split and splinter, responding tersely, "A little!"

"He, like Peter, was tested by Satan. He lost all he had – family, home, wealth, everything. But he did not lose his trust, his love of my Father. When Satan had finished, my Father restored everything Job had lost and much more. The same is true of David. He did many things wrong during his life. At his core, his love for my Father never wavered. Many of David's actions caused great pain to himself and others, and in human terms David paid a heavy price. But deep in his heart he was sorry for what he had done. David's sadness, repentance and love of Yahweh opened the door to his heart. Yahweh was able to discipline him in love, to teach, to prune, making him a humbler, a more understanding and better man, and draw David closer to himself."

"What sort of punishment did David get because I thought he was loved by God and a favourite? Didn't he become the great, great, great grandfather of Jesus?" queried David with a much lighter tone.

Jay's smile was full of joy as he looked at David.

"Yes, he was very dear to my Father's heart from a very early age, but he had to make his own decisions of what to do and what not to do."

"So God didn't guide him and tell him what to do then?" asked David.

"Oh no, that's not my Father's way. The decision to do what pleases or displeases my Father is up to each individual person. David lost his first son with Bathsheba but gained an even greater one later after he had said 'sorry' to my Father. Because of his actions, David's greatest desire, to build a temple for my Father, was given to his son to do. David provided much of the material, but Solomon built the temple."

David, now sounding more childlike with his questions, asked, "Why was not being able to build the temple a punishment for David?"

Jay just smiled. "David's heart was so full of love for my Father, he brought the Ark of the Covenant to Jerusalem, where he wanted to build a grand temple for it. In a great procession, the Ark made its way to Jerusalem. David could not help himself, he sang and danced with so much joy. In some people's eyes he made a complete fool of himself, but he didn't care because he just wanted to praise Yahweh. He wanted to build a beautiful temple to put the Ark in. But because he had been a man of blood and had wrongly used his sword, his power and position, Father said that this desire would not be granted."

"Oh!" said David. "He must have done many things wrong in his life to be punished in such a way by God, mustn't he?"

"Not especially."

David sat rubbing his head, thinking, his face changing expression as each thought passed through his mind. George, on the other hand, sat stiffly upright with a deep frown on his face as he tried to find the words to speak. Looking at George's tort face and blank eyes, Jay gently shook his head and, with a sad expression, looked towards Pete.

"Speak what is on your mind George. Don't try to work out what and how to say it, I'll understand."

"Why didn't God really punish David for the murder, adultery, theft and countless other things he did? And which of the laws had he broken, and is it the number one law?"

Jay just looked at George's eyes, his own wide open like deep fathomless pools, but pools that flowed from him into George.

"Oh George, George! Are you still so full of humankind's hardest thoughts and harshest words? It is only a short time since we shared brotherly love and forgiveness together and you sought new life in me. Do you still cling to the law of punishment and consequence? Have you not understood or let my Father's love in yet? Think back to the deep water of the river."

George looked blankly at Jay not understanding what he had said, his eyebrows creating a symphony of movement as his emotions boiled inside.

"Where is compassion, understanding, a seeking of the truth and, most of all, forgiveness?" questioned Jay.

"But he was in the wrong and deliberate in his actions," exclaimed George.

"And you are not?" queried Jay with a feather-light touch and tone.

George just stopped and looked at Jay, eyes glowing angrily

and dancing in their sockets, with every passing second not knowing what to do or say. Jay rested a hand on George's, squeezing gently as he looked into his eyes.

"In fun, you call the Black Swan the Mucky Duck because it is different to the majority of its kind."

Both George and David frowned, trying to see the relevance of Jay's words.

"All mute swans have black body parts yet in slang you maliciously call a white mute swan a black, sooty foot or a big knob. Each makes poor fun of a different part of the body. The male's black knob sits between his eyes, so he cannot see it. They grow larger during the breeding season to impress the females and indicate strength and virility to all. Power, pride, position, possessions and popularity are like the swan's knob; you do not always see or recognize them, but others can and in many cases are flattered by them as they are seen as wonderful attributes.

"The breaking of laws are also viewed in a similar light and justified by a person to achieve a goal in life. Yahweh gave ten laws, all had the same value. The essence of the ten was simply translated into two: 'to love Yahweh with all your heart', not a little corner of it but all your heart and 'to love your neighbour as much as you love yourself'. If you truly love someone from within your own heart you won't do anything to harm them deliberately. We all make mistakes as we journey through life and it is the loving and forgiving from the heart that makes the journey a joy or a trial.

"What makes the journey more difficult is how we view other people's faults. George, which of two men is guilty of the greater sin: one man who is in a poor marriage and an adulterous relationship, or the one who puts on a show week by week going to church, best suit, doing many good works but does not truly love my Father, only the power, the position and the praise he receives from other church members?"

George sat blank faced, not really wishing to answer. He looked nervously at David as he spoke, as if trying to apologize and say, "I am sorry."

"I suppose the man in the adulterous relationship is the guilty one."

"Why?"

"Well, he is breaking one of God's main laws and it causes great pain and suffering to others. And we take the wedding vows we make before God seriously."

Jay gently shook his head. "Wrong! Both men are committing adultery!"

David spluttered into his glass at Jay's words while George, open-mouthed, said, "How?"

"Think about the Bible and a phrase that is used throughout about the Hebrew nation."

George's face was just a caricature of a question mark as he shook his head.

"The prophets and others referred to them as an 'adulterous nation'. As a nation they did things in the name of Yahweh for show, but did not love Him in their hearts. They did it to show others how wealthy they were, how pious, or to gain praise from their fellow men. They did not love Yahweh with all their heart. Father should be your first love. They loved money, position, power and pride as many do today. If you love them more than Father you are committing adultery."

"Oh, I see," was George's weak reply.

"Do you remember the story of the Pharisees and the woman caught in adultery?"

"Yes, they were going to stone her to death because she had been caught in adultery. But Jesus challenged their motives and they left one by one, and he told her not to commit adultery again."

"Very good!"

George's chest puffed up at Jay's compliment.

"In a very few words you have the essence of the story. The Pharisees loved Yahweh, but as a means to an end; they were in love with power, position, possessions, popularity and pride. They were happy to condemn others who fell short of the laws but not themselves. They considered themselves above the law. The challenge that was put before them was one of honesty and integrity before my Father and their fellow men and women."

"I am not sure I understand what you mean Jay," responded George.

"Me neither, I am totally lost at the moment," commented David.

Jay held his hands up in submission.

"OK, in simple terms the laws come as a package, you cannot pick and mix. All have the same value in Yahweh's eyes as they all relate to our relationship with Him. They also relate to human relationships and help to guide how we should interact."

"Well that bit sounds easy, Jay!" said David.

Jay smiled and continued, "Because they all relate to Yahweh, they all have the same effect in His eyes. They separate you from Him; no one law is greater than another. It does not matter whether you steal, murder, commit adultery or turn your back on Yahweh not loving Him, the effect is the same. In essence, you remove yourself from Yahweh's love. Yahweh does not remove His love, you remove yourself from it! Forgiveness also has a similar but opposite route for each person; in saying sorry, from the heart, you open yourself to Yahweh's love. As the laws are Yahweh's and relate to Him, it is His right and His alone to judge each individual person, and no one else's.

"If you judge a person's actions you are in one sense saying 'I am equal to Yahweh!' You are also saying, as the Pharisees did, I am pure and have committed no sin so I am able to judge another person's sin. When challenged, the older Pharisees knew in their hearts two things; they had sinned during their own lives. And, under the law, both the man and woman caught in adultery should be stoned to death. In leaving they acknowledged that they had not fulfilled the requirements of the law that they were using against the woman. In their hearts they understood this and accepted they were not able to pass judgment on the woman."

"Now I begin to understand," said George. "I suppose that is why Jesus said 'don't judge or you will be judged by the same law and you should love and forgive your enemies.'"

Jay and Pete had smiles that beamed out and both nodded their heads in agreement.

"George, in acknowledging this, do you not think you should put it into practice in your life?" questioned Jay.

The question caused George's countenance to change in an instance with a frown that deepened second by second.

"I do!" was his sharp response.

"Do you?" queried Jay.

George frowned even more.

"Yes I do! I forgive people lots of times for the things they do wrong, we talk them through and apologize to each other. As a Christian man it is my duty, it is what is asked of and expected of me!"

"True, but do you forgive a person from the heart?"

"I'd like to think so," George paused for a moment. "Yes, I do forgive them from the heart!"

"And what about David?"

George looked at David, eyeball to eyeball.

"Of course I forgive David, he's my best mate!"

David smiled back at George.

"Thanks for the vote of confidence George."

Jay looked straight at George, whose eyes became as sharp as pins as they looked into the deep pools of Jay's.

"So you forgive all David's sins from your heart, especially those you know about?"

"Yes of course I do, I have already said so," George retorted, with a very hard tone to his voice.

"So you forgive him his adultery with Simone?"

George turned to stone, fixed and rigid, his colour that of freshly cut chalk.

"Have you not understood our time by the river George?" questioned Jay.

George's eyes looked straight at Jay's, initially, with a haughty look of pride, position and power. The internal dam of self-will began to crack. The five 'P's began to slowly drain away, enabling the rock of humbleness in his heart to be seen. Slowly, very slowly, his head dropped. Jay's gentle loving steady gaze continued to look at the top of George's head.

"George!" said Jay. "It is true to say David has relationship problems that will cause him and others a great deal of turmoil and heart searching. The people involved are of concern to me because promises have been broken and love is being replaced by mistrust, joy by anger, sharing by possessiveness."

David's head snapped upwards in response to Jay's words. His hand jerked in reflex, sending his glass flying, spilling his drink. David's eyes were wide open like saucers, yet filled with hurt, anger, amazement and the unspoken question of 'how dare you'. Time seemed to slow as the two men looked at each other, eyes locked, as the tranquility of love in Jay began to triumph over pride and all its friends. Jay broke the stunned silence.

"Pete, can you get some more drinks please."

"No problem," came the reply from a face that had a very know-it-all smile.

David stammered, "How do you…?"

Jay's hand reassuringly touched David's, cutting off any more words. Jay continued to focus on George.

"You are the one I came to speak to George, as you are the one that is truly divorced from Our Father."

George's head flicked up and round as if attached to a giant spring, his face losing its pained expression.

"No I am not!" was his terse response.

"George, open your heart as you did by the river. Pride and position blind you and hold you captive. Let my love in, to the deeper reaches of your heart, so that you may be a real shepherd of Yahweh's flock. Like David, 'a man after His heart' and not human reasoning. Pride and its family are the ones that build walls; barriers that cause you to be divorced from Yahweh and me. But, if you let me into your heart, we can dismantle those walls together and be as one."

George whimpered like a distressed child.

"But I am frightened and don't know what to do!"

Jay took his hand, saying softly, "You do know! I, Jesus, will help you as I have with countless other children. Fix the eyes of your heart on me and not on the ways, the words and requirements that the world imposes on you!"

At Jay's words, David's eyes popped wide open, reducing to slits of doubt and incredulity.

"George, at the river bank you began a journey. The journey of loving My Father with all your heart."

George looked at Jay blankly, expressionless, head moving up and down, micro millimetre slowly in acknowledgement.

"To be truly and wholly forgiven for your sins you have to forgive from your heart. Your Pharisees' type of love for Yahweh is turning slowly into true love, but it needs to show true and real love and forgiveness to others. You are trying to fulfil the easiest and yet the hardest of all the laws; loving God with an open and unrestricted heart! To do that you cannot judge as others would judge and punish, but forgive David his sin and all the other Davids and Janes in this world from your heart."

George, motionless, just looked at David. His eyes began to glisten and sparkle. A single tear rolled down his cheek.

Chapter 12

I Don't Understand? -
It's NOT IDEAL

Pete appeared through the pub garden door carrying a tray with tea and coffee pots and a plate full of home-made scones. Placing the try on the table with a 'this should keep us going', he looked at his companions with a wide open satisfied smile, finally resting on George.

With words like the gentle loving purr of a cat, he said to George, "Now you know what it's like to look into those eyes!"

George just looked blankly. But slowly, his memory searching reaching back to what had been said earlier, a radiant smile appeared with the words, "Yes I do!"

Three of them began to tuck into the scones and hot drinks, but David just hung his head.

"Come on David," encouraged Pete. "The tea and coffee's great and the scones are to die for. They are gorgeous!"

David's head hung down, his mind confused and in turmoil as he unconsciously rolled a scone over and over. Looking at Pete and pointing roughly at Jay, he spat out, "I suppose if he says he is Jesus you are Peter the fisherman!" Pete just smiled.

"I am, but you can call me Simon or Peter, or Pete is just fine if you are more comfortable with that! I am just an ordinary man like you!"

"Yes right!" was David's sarcastic response.

A quiet yet uncomfortable calm covered the table as the two friends tried to come to terms with what had been revealed. David's rock-like face looked at Jay.

"I don't understand! I am not sure I believe you are who you say you are, but if you are; answer me this! Who is Yahweh, who is God and who is this Father? I thought God was God yet you seem to use these different names in the conversation as if they are related to the same being?"

Jay's simple "They are!" brought a deep stillness over the whole table. He continued, "The name Yahweh is the special name the ancient Hebrews used and still use for God Almighty. In simple terms, the sovereign name of God among all his other names."

"All His other names?" questioned David with incredulity in his voice.

Jay smiled. "Many of the Hebrew names of God speak of His different royal attributes, holy, almighty, creator, strong, wise, loving, forgiving, compassionate and so on. The word God, however, is a more generalized term that combines all the individual names into one. Using these two ways of speaking about and to Yahweh, humankind generally holds itself, but not all, at a distance from God.

"In Holy Scriptures the words of Samuel, Isaiah, Elijah and David and others indicate a far more personal and intimate relationship with Him. The term Father reflects that personal and intimate relationship with God. Yahweh, God and Father are the same loving person. It is a person's perception that changes. Many begin their journey with the creator or sovereign attributes. As they learn more about Him, they open their hearts to Him. As they draw nearer to Him they begin to understand His loving and compassionate nature."

David butted in! "Are you saying I have to learn the Bible

and the great thick tomes you see in libraries to know God?"

"No!" was Jay's emphatic response.

"Well what then!"

"It's a beginning!"

"If it's a beginning, how do I…?

Jay raised both hands to bring to an end David's harsh outburst. Pausing, for a few moments, agitation cooled and a peaceful atmosphere returned.

"You don't read a book to tell your heart who or how to love someone! It is something that just grows from inside. The same is true when you love Yahweh. There will be a grain of sand in your heart, a question, an irritation, a desire to find out that seemingly comes from nowhere, wanting to know more about Yahweh. You read the Bible and other books to try and satisfy the irritation. That produces knowledge, which gives direction. It is a joy and uplifting to many, but it is not the final chapter."

David groaned, struggling to listen and understand Jay's words.

"That grain of sand, that irritation, wants to produce a pearl of love in your heart that no book learning can give you. The irritation you and George feel is that grain of sand trying to become a pearl. Your love, George's love, is struggling to be free, but history, your human perceptions, are trying to prevent that happening. Yahweh loves you intimately and He wants you to love Him just as intimately."

"So how do I achieve this intimate relationship?" queried David.

"By holding little or nothing back in your life and building in your heart a desire for a truly personal intimate relation-ship with Yahweh. Sometimes the use of one of the exclusive names helps you gain an insight into your relationship and perspective of God."

"I am not sure I understand what you mean about the names and our relationship and perspective of God?" queried David.

Jay smiled.

"The heart is softening and wants to know. A very simple generalization would be to say Yahweh was and still is to many a very special term used for God that reaches back to the time of the creation and law. God, singular or with its adjectives, God Almighty, Loving God and Living God, are some of the terms used in the everyday vernacular. With these names a person can know God, and many do. But a person's relationship is sometimes stilted because with these and similar names they hold God at arm's length, or become a practitioner of the law, or holiness, or another small aspect of humankind's relationship with God. To call God 'Father' changes the relationship perspective between God and humankind because of its natural commonplace paternal use. Think of the most common prayer I taught. It begins with the words 'Our Father'. In saying 'Our Father' you are saying 'I am a child of God', or 'God is my father or my 'daddy'. To say God is your 'daddy' is the nearest modern translation to the Hebrew word that was used for both God and an earthly Father, 'abba'. The two words, daddy and abba, suggest an intimate relationship that is formalized in the word 'Father'."

"That's amazing! To think God actually wants to have an intimate and personal relationship with me even though I am in a relationship with Simone."

A profound silence descended over the table as David's words of hope and 'confession' settled in their hearts and minds. With an anguished wail in his voice, David continued as the realities and condemnation of humankind burst through the peace.

"But how CAN God love me when the Ten Commandments condemn me, as will many of those who call themselves friends. And I don't see how they all can be of the same value. If you ask anyone, there is a hierarchy and often adultery is at the top of the list, above stealing and murder!"

David's body slumped down, face knotted as if in pain looking like a long dried prune.

Jay's hand reached across and gently rested on David's. His hand just remained still, unmoving like a slab of meat on a butcher's block.

"In Yahweh's eyes, all the laws are equal and have equal need of loving discipline. As you have rightly said, it is in the eyes of humankind that each law has a different value and different punishment."

David looked at Jay with blank lifeless eyes. Motionless, set as stones in an alabaster face.

"It is true what you have said; adultery is often at the top of the list in the eyes of humankind. It often affects a wide circle of people, as does murder or robbery or slander, but they seem to be generally forgiven more readily. Everyone breaks the laws in their heart; others in deed. Other law breakers hide their indiscretion from humankind, but they cannot hide it from my Father. Similarly, in human society laws are broken out of expediency or because they are not relevant in today's world. Yahweh wants all humankind to be like Him, compassionate, understanding, but most of all forgiving. In Yahweh's eyes you have committed adultery, but so has George. Both of you are guilty of the same sin, same wrong action, and therefore have the same need for repentance."

George's eyes popped open as if he had been prodded by a hot poker, his mouth wide open, jaw moving up and down soundlessly trying to protest his innocence.

"If you are sorry from your heart, and I know you are, Yahweh will help you and guide you through to a new life, a new relationship."

A quiet calm enveloped the companions at the table as an early morning mist hovered over a pond.

David's eyes, however, began to glisten and as they did so they became as hard as diamonds. Looking straight at Jay, hard faced and with a razor edge to his voice, he said, "You may say you are Jesus and have many wonderful words. But how do you know about me and who gave you the right to make it public knowledge?"

"I know many things about you that are not ideal, but as to making the information public knowledge, George in his heart already knew. Pete knew before you met him on the river bank!"

"What?" squeaked David.

"How on earth could they know? I have never said anything to George and I only met Pete today." Jay looked into David's eyes, with sadness in his own, yet filled with understanding and compassion. He reached out a hand again to hold and reassured David. David's hand recoiled as if attached to an over-taught spring, snapping back from Jay's.

"We all do things that are not of the best and which we are not proud of, but if you ask for forgiveness and mean it from your heart my Father will forgive you."

"That's as may be," snapped David. "But George and many other people will not forgive me, no matter what I say or the circumstances…"

Jay's hand raised, stopping David.

"Judgemental attitudes and the lack of forgiving by others is one of humankind's greatest faults."

"So you agree then?" said David butting in.

"Sadly yes, but not all are like that."

George looked very uncomfortable, keeping his head turned away from David and wriggling in his seat as though a nail had suddenly pushed up from below. Pete, on the other hand, had a sad expression on his face but, like the tear on a clown's mask, a smile was only a silly word away from being a rib-tickling laugh.

"David! We all make mistakes and do things that are not right and hurt others and ourselves. So don't be too hard on yourself," interjected Pete.

"How do you know? Have you committed adultery and been publicly humiliated?"

"No, not in the way you mean!" was the quiet response.

"I have done things I am not proud of and for which I am still condemned and ridiculed by some people. But I cannot do anything about their thoughts and actions. I can only pray for them; that they will forgive me as my Lord Jesus did."

"That Christian bit is all very well but I have got to live in the real world. In my job I would be fired because of protocol if people knew about my failing marriage and relationship with Simone. Half the truth would come out, people would make up the missing parts and put the wrong interpretation on the situation."

Jay asked in a sympathetic tone, "Why? Why would half the truth be wrong and what is there to hide. Wouldn't the whole truth and situation be better spoken of openly?"

David's expression was blank and ashen-faced, with eyes that just seemed to be fixed on a point somewhere in outer space. The other three just sat quietly drinking their coffee and tea, waiting. David drew in a deep shuddering breath, which caused the others to sit up, focusing their attention expectantly on him. He sighed deeply and settled near to the table like a balloon that was deflating. The others just looked at one another, not sure what to say or do, how to break the silence, or how to encourage him to trust and speak openly.

David, head near to the table and speaking as if to the table, said, "Can I trust you to say nothing to anyone else if I tell you a pitiful story, especially you George?"

George sputtered out, "Of course you can."

"I really mean it George, you know Anne and many of my friends. There's one or two who would love to make great scandal out of my situation, making it sound much worse, and certainly in one case he'd love to 'leak' it to the papers."

"David, I know I am a bit of an idiot at times, but trust me, I consider you my best friend and would not and do not want to cause you harm. What you say here, now, will stay here."

David and George locked eyes, time stood still for an eternity as they sought truthful confirmation of the spoken words in each other's eyes.

"That's the first time you have said you think of me as your best friend!"

"I have thought of you as that for a long time. Didn't you realize! Didn't all the fun times and times chatting together give you a hint of how I felt about you?"

David, with a pained tone in his voice said, "No! You never said or made it clear. I thought I was on the edge of the crowd, one that needed saving, with all the church people you have come round."

George's arm went around David's shoulders, lifting him from the table. He drew him close and held him firmly.

"I am sorry I never said anything, never made it clear how I felt. I have loved you as if you were my brother for a long time. My church friends are just that, friends. They come and go. The relationship with most is shallow, no roots, only Sunday mornings and the odd midweek event to draw us together. But with you it's different."

David, eyes filling with tears, responded, "Do you really mean that?"

"Yes, I do!" came the firm response.

Silence came as a warm embrace that covered all, protecting them from the world and giving time for the two friends to wallow in the knowledge and new found depth of their friendship. Minutes ticked by until David coughed as he tried to stifle a laugh that had begun in his toes. He failed miserably and spluttered everywhere. Like a genie leaping out of its bottle, it infected the others in a microsecond and all were roaring with laughter as they enjoyed and shared in a love realized. The tea, coffee and scones became an impromptu celebration along with the laughter, gentle banter and the teenage giggles as the two friends looked at each other with very new eyes.

Looking at George eye to eye with an expression that said, "I need to say this to show you I do trust you, make things right between us," David said, "I do love Anne, but for a long while we've just seemed to…"

David looked to the sky for inspiration. George, Jay and Pete looked encouragingly at David, but not wishing to break his thoughts kept silent.

"Just seemed… to live together as colleagues. You know, doing the general mundane things that need to be done around the house. But without any spark, no 'I want to do this or that to please her'. We care for each other in a practical sense. We do jobs for each other. We say we love each other, but the words are dry and fragile as long dead wood. It's as though the heart we had for each other has died. I have often looked at Barbara and yourself and wished we could find the same light, warm happiness. I just never seemed to be able to find the right time or catch Anne in the right mood to talk. We would just sit for hours, days, without really speaking. Seeing you and Barbara and many others like you chattering away, being silly together, I became envious and a need grew in me to find that sort of happiness for myself. For a long, long time I kept forcing it down. I may not be a Christian like you, but I wanted to try and keep my marriage together."

Jay's gentle grasp of George's hand and tiny shake of his head stopped him from speaking.

David continued, "As time went by, my heart became warmer, more alive when others flattered me. Sadly it made going home all the harder. Anne didn't seem to notice, or care, or say anything, just a grey nothingness. When Simone began to help me at work nothing happened to begin with, we were just working colleagues. We started doing creative work, brainstorming and the like. It was like..." David again paused looking for inspiration.

"Like we were like two pop bottles. She shook me and I exploded with ideas. I shook her and she exploded with ideas. Those times were magical and our bosses thought it was great as so many good and commercially productive ideas came from those times.

"I don't know when or how it changed, but it did. In my heart, I knew it was wrong, I was a married man, but the happiness I so longed for was there in Simone making me laugh and laughing with me. I'd go home to Anne and look at the woman I had loved becoming, in my eyes, more and more grey. I'd tear my heart out at home saying 'it's your duty to stay', but the greyness just grew darker. I cannot see a life of happiness now with Anne, only with Simone. I keep trying to summon up the courage to try and tell her 'I want a divorce'. As soon as I feel ready to tell her, something happens or I look at her and guilt comes over me and I can't say anything because of guilt and remorse. It's as though I am on a set of scales. At one end is duty and Anne and at the other is Simone and the happiness I longed for."

David looked at George and, with a great wail in his voice, cried, "What do I do? I created this mess by letting my emotions run away, by not speaking to Anne and letting things build up, but I want happiness, not stale duty. How can I get out of this mess?"

George just looked at David with tears trickling down his cheeks and he mouthed the words,

"I am so sorry, I did not know. You seemed to be happy at home to me. But what to do next I have no idea."

Pete looked at David with compassionate eyes, gently shaking his head.

"David, do you think your relationship with Anne could be rebuilt?"

David just looked at Pete, shaking a face that was full of sadness and uncertainty.

"My best friend forgave me after I denied him. Having said sorry, our relationship grew from strength to strength, changing my life in so many ways."

David remained unmoving, blank, lifeless, hearing but seemingly not comprehending the words. Jay's hands clasped David's, firmly yet with tenderness and understanding.

"David," said Jay, in a tender soft voice as though a whisper had kissed his cheek.

"Yahweh understands your dilemma and will continue to love you no matter what you decide to do. What you have done and what you may do in the future is not ideal, but Yahweh understands. He also loves Anne as she has her story to tell of long nights on her own, business trips, dinner parties with nothing in common with the other guests. Relationships can grow cold for many different reasons, some can be rebuilt, whereas with others it is better to say it is finished and to part, but in a loving way."

"But Anne will be gutted whatever I say."

"That is true," continued Jay. "It is all part of the effect the breakdown of your relationship will have."

"What about work?" whined David.

"Work will say words they do not mean. They will threaten and demand but do nothing because you have a gift they want to exploit."

"What about our friends?" interjected David.

Jay continued, "Sadly they will take sides. Some will condemn, others will shun you, still others will be there for you but at arm's length and a small number will stand by you, but only a small number."

"It sounds as if I am to be condemned whatever I do. If I stay with Anne I condemn myself to a very uncertain relationship, which could improve or just stay in its greyness. To make a new life with Simone is obviously uncertain, but that life could be a joy-filled life."

"Well," said Jay. "You understand much of the two roads that lay before you. As you have said, from your perspective neither is wholly ideal as each has its negatives and positives. The question you have to ask and answer for yourself is which road you believe is the right one for you?"

In a dejected voice, David said, "I suppose you are right. It's my decision to make and whichever I make I am going to be on my own and in some way in the wrong!"

"In human terms, you may be right," said Jay with a sad tone to his voice as David's eyes hardened and his countenance took on a very dejected air.

"But…!" continued Jay with a radiant expression, as though he had the solution, "No matter which road you choose, if you and George try in your hearts to trust in my Father's guiding Spirit and love for you, even though you are uncertain about Him, He will be with you, supporting and caring towards you, Anne and Simone and the many millions in similar dilemmas."

Chapter 13

Love over Law

George looked at Jay with an exasperated and taught face.

"I can understand your reasoning in saying that David has committed adultery and may ultimately be divorced, but why do you associate me with his faults?" pointing rudely at David, who recoiled backwards as if George's finger was a loaded gun!

Jay just looked at George with a sombre face. He waited quietly, letting the hard words evaporate and peace to wrap around all at the table, before continuing.

"Think back to the beginning George, to the time when the law was given to the Hebrew nation. They had become dissatisfied with God's provision and care, wanting more. Dissension had also crept into some hearts that wanted power and personal glorification. Out of love, Yahweh gave Moses ten simple laws to live by and encourage, enabling His children to live in harmony. If the laws are embraced in love they do bring harmony to the one and to a nation. Sadly, humankind has taken those laws to itself as a burden and not a gift. As a burden, the laws only illuminated humankind's inability to keep them. Like any law, they require justice when broken. They also require the law breaker to pay a penalty when the law is broken."

George's face was filled by a scowl, but he was thoughtful nevertheless, while David's eyes were wide open trying to assimilate Jay's words. Pete, on the other hand, had a quiet smile on his face as he gently sipped his tea.

"What humankind then and now fails to recognize is that the laws also relate to their relationship in the spiritual with Yahweh. If you say with a flourish and all verbal sincerity to another person, 'I love Yahweh', but do not mean it, Yahweh knows you do not mean it while the other person, because of your sincere words, may consider you a wonderful God-fearing man. Yahweh sees into the deepest recesses of all your heart; so you can hide nothing from Him. He will see and recognize your words, your deeds for what they really are. In the same way, if you say in your heart with real sincerity and love of Him, 'I am sorry for what I have done', He will forgive you, no matter what humankind may say or think!"

George's eyes and face hardened as his mind was trying in a defensive way to understand what Jay was saying.

"The Pharisee, like yourself George, could never see his own faults because pride covered them over and made them acceptable."

"What on earth do you mean?" exclaimed George.

"You are a learned man George but, like so many, you still don't understand or see your own need of a penitent and contrite, but most of all loving, heart because you hide your own faults and sins, in the way you interpret and use the law. David's sin will be before him for some time. For some, his sin will never go away. David will have to wrestle with what to do and accept the consequences of his decision. Your sin, your divorce, George is the same as the Hebrew nation's."

David's eyes popped wide open for a spilt second in acknowledgment of Jay's words. Just as quickly, his head fell as the realization and meaning of those words in his life hit home!

Jay raised his hand to stop George as he began to splutter out protestations of his innocence.

"All children are 'mucky ducks' in God's eyes. Each has faults unique to them that make each mucky! George, you serve yourself under a cloak of serving Yahweh and by your actions and the intentions of your heart divorce yourself from Him. Like King David and many of the priests of old, you serve yourself in the power, the glorification of self, you weald week by week and as you preach, but not fulfilling your own words in your life. It is also in the way you absorb the flattery of others as they speak of your position, your status in society, in the prestige you seek when at functions. You revel in the glory yourself. You do not give the glory back to Yahweh and you do not truly nurture the flock in your care because the love in your heart is still only lukewarm. The pride of humankind hides all these things from you, and the truth. It makes excuses for all the other flaws and draws together all their strands like a spider's web. But, as with King David, forgiveness races quickly after a penitent heart."

George's countenance was brittle as lead glass and as white as chalk, yet strangely fluid as expression after expression flowed across his face.

David leapt to George's defence.

"George is nothing like that. He is a good man and cares about people."

"In George's heart he knows my words are true and his love is lukewarm."

"What?" exclaimed David.

"Did George not say only moments ago that his relationship with his church friends was shallow and had no roots?"

Jay paused. The words, like clothes in a drier, tumbled around in David's mind.

"Yes he did, but I don't think he meant them as you are portraying them!"

"David, when George spoke of your relationship he was speaking from his heart. He was speaking from the same heart when he spoke of those he has been commissioned to care for."

"Oh!" commented David.

"You mean he really meant what he said about me!"

"Yes I did!" interjected George, stung into action by the discussion going on around him that snapped a guitar string of a nerve inside his mind. Jay seemingly ignored George and continued speaking, to David's confusion. In reality, he was speaking as much to George as David.

"George has, with others, the pastoral care of Yahweh's flock, which needs much help. He is often as shallow as they are and all have hearts filled with stone. When George allowed his heart to be filled with love he became as a good shepherd and cared for the young lamb in distress, you David."

David's eyes became the size of dinner plates, looking as if they were about to fall out of their sockets.

"If George allowed the Spirit of Yahweh to be in his heart, all the time, he would realize how needy the flock is that he has been given to serve. And it is to serve; not to lead, not to lord it over them, not to teach a theology, but to guide, to enable them on their journey. To be a channel of Yahweh's love and as a flock, together, find love and peace in Yahweh's home as His sons and daughters. That also includes you, David. It also requires you to help George."

David, with a timid voice, questioned, "I know I am in distress, but how can George help me? And more to the point, how can I help him? The Church, and George as one of its leaders, will and should condemn me because of my actions!"

Jay, shaking his head and with eyes filling with tears, looked steadily at both George and David.

"I gave my life that the Church might have life, my love that they might share that love with others. I gave my selflessness that they might show compassion and forgiveness to others. My Father's pure love is so great he gave everything as a free gift to humankind. His 'grace' was poured out through me without any preconditions or limit.

"However, humankind is becoming selfish once again: trusting in their own ability. They take my Father's laws and use them as a weapon against each other, much as they did all those years ago, and fail to realize or acknowledge that they too are breaking the same laws. Where compassion, understanding, forgiveness and love are needed, they condemn, punish, isolate and some say, 'you are a sinner, God can no longer use you'. In making that statement they are, in word, making themselves equal to Yahweh! They are passing judgement on another when they too will have many hidden flaws. They forget how many flawed people my Father has used through time.

"Many servant children come to Him with penitent broken hearts to find He has already forgiven and restored them through me! Still others have compiled their own new laws, which put additional burdens on the backs of His children. With these they intend to control, to isolate from each other and from my Father's wider family. But His love, His Spirit, is greater than any law and he continues to draw His children together and to himself. What many children forget is, in Yahweh's eyes you are all 'Mucky Ducks', but all is far from lost. My Father loved you so much that instead of the justice and punishment required by the law He gave you me, as a gift, through which all your mistakes are washed away. His gift of grace is there for all who look to and accept me in their hearts. Yahweh looks at you though me and sees only a beautiful child. All your mistakes: past, present and future are forgiven through me; enabling each and everyone who loves me to be accepted as a son or daughter."

Chapter 14

A Loving Father

George nodded agreement to Jay's words but, with a condescending voice, asked, "What you have said is all very well, but are you still suggesting that God cares for David more than me? After all, I care for David as a friend, but also in a different way as he is now a sinner. Should God not love me more so that I can help David and help prepare him for eternal life?"

David recoiled, gasping at George's blunt words.

Jay gently shook his head.

"Yahweh loves all His children, no matter who or what they are or have done."

"Yes, I know that!" said George butting in. "But, love has its limits and wrong has to be punished in some way!"

"George, let me open your mind to two stories you will be familiar with; The Good Shepherd and The Prodigal Son."

George just grunted an acknowledgement.

"Which of the sheep did the shepherd love the most? The one lost or the flock in the pen?" George thought for a short while before spitting out his terse reply. "I suppose the one that was lost as he had to spend extra time and effort to find it."

"Which of the two sons did the father love the most?"

"Oh!" exclaimed George, "That's easy, the one that left home because when he came back he was spoilt rotten by his father, feast, clothes, a ring and so on."

"What would you say if I said they were all loved equally?"

George frowned.

"I would say you were wrong. How could they be loved equally when so much time and effort was spent on the single sheep and the wayward son?"

Jay sipped his tea and, putting his cup down, looked at Pete with an eye that had a twinkle in it that suggested 'I know what I am doing, I have been here before!'

Sue was going about her duties, taking orders and collecting used crockery and glasses. Unseen by George and David, she approached the table. Jay smiled encouragingly at her, as though inviting her to listen as he continued to speak.

"The shepherd loved all his sheep equally, what differed was his concern. When they arrived home, the shepherd's concern was for the flock. They were put into the pen so that they were protected from harm, safe for the coming night. The shepherd's concern then, and only then, turned to the needs of the sheep that had strayed. The shepherd hadn't left the flock on the hills to search for the one. With the flock protected, then and only then did the shepherd walk back to the grazing area. As he searched he would have increased the search area until he found the lost sheep. Having found it, he was happy; the sheep was still alive and hopefully would learn a lesson and not wander off on its own again. Many people call themselves 'God's Children' but wander away to do their own thing with no thought for the pain they cause Yahweh in doing so. My Father's love is boundless and He cares for the whole flock just as much as the ones that have wandered away."

"But, the sheep that wandered away was not sorry," interjected George.

"That's true George, but don't take the stories literally. Look beyond. Look at the shepherd's concern, his joy, his willingness to search for the one no matter what the cost to himself. You, and many Davids, Sues and Williams, like you, stray. All are searched for and found at no cost to themselves."

"So how does that tie in with the Prodigal Son, because he was sorry when he came back and his father had not gone out to search for him!" insisted George.

"That is true," confirmed Jay.

"So how does that tie up then?" said George with an insistent note in his voice.

"They 'tie up', as you put it, in the concern and love the father had for his two children, sons or daughters."

Jay continued with a quiet, instructive tone.

"Firstly, the father loved the younger son enough to let him go and explore life, even though he had his own fears and misgivings."

"But, the Bible…," shrieked George as if he was in pain.

Jay raised a hand to still the unspoken words.

"Look in, look beyond with your heart at the words," was Jay's response.

"The father loved his child enough to let him go! His concern, fears and misgivings are seen in the looking day after day for his child's return. He could do nothing for his child so far away, but that did not stop him loving and being concerned for their welfare."

David spoke up in a timid sounding voice. "That sounds like a loving parent to me George."

"Me too!"

George and David spun round, surprised by Sue's words.

"I had never considered the cost of leaving home, Mum and Dad, in those terms. They have always been there for me, through thick and thin, and never had any hesitation when I was down and needed help."

Jay smiled at Sue who, realizing she was now the centre of

attention, blushed a pale rose pink. Stammering, she asked if any more refreshments were required. An order for more tea and cake was given. As Sue was about to leave, Jay held her eyes for a few moments with his own.

"Sue's words encapsulate her modern day loving relationship with her parents, but also those between the father and prodigal son."

"What about the older brother, Jay? What happened in his relationship?"

Jay smiled at David and continued.

"The older brother inherited and ran the estate under his father's guidance. His father held the estate 'in trust', as many do today. On his death, it would pass automatically to his eldest son. The father loved and trusted the eldest son so much that allowed him to care for and run the estate long before he needed to."

George grumbled quietly, like a bear that had not eaten, as he digested the words before speaking.

"If that's the case, why did the father throw such a lavish party for the younger son and never for the older son?"

Jay's expression was halfway between a frown and smile as he spoke quietly to George.

"When a loved one returns from an extended absence is it not normal to celebrate their return and show your love and release the pent up concern inside? The father did nothing more than that. The celebrations may sound lavish, but are only appropriate to the son's position as the son of a landowner."

"Oh!" exclaimed George more quietly.

"But, why had no party been given for the eldest son?"

Jay continued, "The eldest son, if he had thought about his situation, owned everything! He could have had a party at any time! The elder son, however, was ensnared by rules, laws, tradition and his interpretation of them. This disabled him so much that the true potential of the gift he had been given was not recognized."

David looked at Jay. "Are you saying that it was the elder son's fault that he did not have a party of his own?"

Jay paused for a moment before responding.

"Fault is the wrong word, its meaning too harsh, too definite in meaning. It is better to say the older son misunderstood and was misled. The law, tradition are very black and white, hiding the loving intensions of the father from the eyes and heart of the elder son. He had not grasped, not understood, the extent of the father's loving gift."

"Oh!" exclaimed David.

"That paints a very different picture and puts the blame elsewhere."

Jay frowned deeply.

"The requirements, the letter of the law, had been lovingly fulfilled by the father. The word 'blame' again looks back to the nature of the law. It wants to point a finger, to make an excuse, to exact a penalty, to say you are the one who is in the wrong and who caused the upset. If there was any wrong it was in the literal and historic interpretation of the law."

David raised a finger and began speaking excitedly in great haste.

"Are we like the eldest son, misinterpreting the old laws, and is that true of all the laws? For instance, we all live under the Ten Commandments in some way or another and get severely punished if we break them. You said the father had fulfilled the requirements; do you mean paid for, in full? But, which law, all or some? Who is the father figure, God?"

Pete smiled at Jay, "The doors to a new heart have been unlocked!"

Jay smiled back and continued, "So many questions. The father in both stories loves all the sheep and both sons equally. His 'concern', however, is for the one most in need, but not at the expense of the other. The flock is made safe before seeking the lost. The elder son is given, and acknowledged as heir to, all the father's property. The gift of the father to the younger, then, was modest but in keeping with the younger son's position on his return. Today George, when you said goodbye to Barbara you showed your concern for her by saying, 'Safe journey and happy landings'. Your concern for her safety and love was expressed in those words as she left your immediate protection. When David invited you to the Black Swan, your concern changed and focused on him."

George's face was a picture of question marks as he mouthed silently, 'How did you know that?'

Jay continued, "Your love for Barbara has not changed, grown any less, because your concern has been focused on David. Are you beginning to understand and know the difference in your heart between love and concern? Know too in your heart that Yahweh's love for you is as rich as it is for David and all His other children, regardless of what you call status or position in life. He is concerned for your well-being just as He is for David's, in ways that are unique to each of you."

George shook his head slightly as a question formed in his mind.

"The Bible tells us Jesus had his favourites and loved one over another! Didn't he have a favourite disciple, John, who he loved more than the others? And, didn't John have a special place at the last supper next to Jesus so he was able to rest his head on his chest? And, didn't Jesus entrust the care of his mother to John?"

Jay gently nodded his head in agreement. "It is written as you have summarized."

George's face was even more a picture of triumph with a very smug smile.

"But, and there is one big but and several interpretations and reasons for what was done."

A frown flashed across George's face as Jay continued.

"The source is not in doubt, nor the words used. However, the interpretation of the original phrase may have been misunderstood. All the disciples were loved equally, but in different ways as each had different needs and interpretations of love that were personal. One may have been comfortable with an open kiss or embrace, another with a personal quiet intimate time. Each would find the other person's way of expressing love uncomfortable, embarrassing, preventing love to be truly embraced."

"That's a very good way of putting it Jay," interjected David. "I would have great difficulty with the first, especially if it was a man!"

George nodded in agreement but made no comment.

"Each of the disciples had unique talents, which were used by Yahweh and me. Judas was good with figures and the care of money, which is why he was given charge of our communal purse. Peter was a good leader, able to make decisions, encourage others and, in time, became an inspiring orator. John was a quiet studious sort of man with a deep spiritual mind. And yes! He was the type of person you would trust the care of a loved one to. His deep spiritual mind gave him a special insight to the words of Yahweh, which helped many. None were loved any more than another, just differently."

"That's all fine in theory, but are you saying in Yahweh's eyes I am equal to David, who is a sinner in the fullest sense of the word because he is committing adultery? The requirements of God's Law have to be fulfilled and justice and punishment meted out!"

Quietly but firmly, Jay asked, "And what about forgiveness, compassion, understanding and love? Did I not fulfil the requirements of the law, once for all time on the cross?"

George just sat there stunned, frowning at Jay's words.

David looked deeply saddened and shocked at his friend's words. "Even you, in your heart and now out loud, condemn me George! I had hoped that with what you have been saying you at least would understand and stand by me. What chance do I have if you run hot and cold when the rest of the community find out? I will be friendless, on my own with no one to turn to!"

Jay reached out and gently took David's hand. "I will always be your friend, as will George when he lets the truth burn brightly in his heart."

"You know the story of the woman caught in adultery. George can play the part of the adulterous man and David the woman."

George sniggered.

"The Pharisees paraded the woman before the crowd and me seeking a guilty judgement and the sentence as prescribed. Their hope to entrap me was futile and their own weapon, the law, used to highlight their own poor ways. Her sin according to the law had been pronounced and the required sentence sought. If those in authority required it, like the woman, David could be paraded before the people, vilified, sentenced and shunned as an outcast."

David spluttered into his tea, looking at Jay with a very pained face. Jay smiled at David reassuringly.

"Don't worry, it is unlikely to happen. The woman's fault,

indiscretion, was there for all to examine. But adultery takes two people! What of the man involved? Was he any less guilty than she? Why was he not brought before the people and me?"

George's face was a kaleidoscope of emotions as he tried to embrace what Jay had said. "The Pharisees knew the requirements of the law. Because of their own willful desires, they presented only half the truth. To pass any judgement would have been wrong."

"That is my greatest fear," said David. "That only half the truth would come out and people would pass judgement regardless. What was the other half of the truth and did it come out?"

Jay smiled at David.

"It did! In our story, the indiscretion of the man, played by George, was not spoken of, nor was he brought before the people with the woman. He was as guilty as she. George, in fact, is no different. He has indiscretions including adultery that are hidden away."

George exclaimed, "What?"

As his hand hit the table, making the tea cups shake, Pete grinned. "That caught a raw nerve in you George. Don't worry, what we know, what is said here, remains here!"

"George, you know now your adultery is in your actions towards Yahweh and the way you care for his children and not with another person," said Jay reassuringly.

"Under the law, however, both are considered as adultery. In the same way, under the law both the man and woman were guilty of adultery. Both should have been brought before the people and judged. In bringing only the woman, the Pharisees had not fulfilled the requirements of the law. They were manipulating the law to their own selfish ends. In doing this they themselves were outside the law. When challenged, the older Pharisees acknowledged their wrongdoing, their guilt, and did not condemn the woman. In the same way, a person should look into their own heart before condemning another."

Chapter 15

Grace and Love

"George! May I speak too and enable your heart to embrace another point of view and a more loving way?" asked Jay in a gentle tone.

A simple nod of the head was George's only response.

"I know you are familiar with the words of John."

George nodded in agreement as his eyes opened a little wider as familiar ground beckoned.

"In his first chapter, John speaks of the 'Word', its closeness to God and creation."

George nodded in affirmation and sat more upright as his interest was being fully engaged.

"The Word is often translated into the name and person of Jesus, God's beloved Son. In chapter three, John talks of God loving the world so much that he gave his son..."

George interrupted enthusiastically.

"That's John three, verse sixteen, 'For God so loved the world that he gave his one and only Son, that whoever believes in Him shall not perish but have eternal life'. A powerful verse full of God's love and promise!"

Jay's smile was radiant. He continued.

"I would like you to hold several verses and ideas together: From chapter one, 'In the beginning was the Word', and 'Through Him all things were made'. From chapter three, 'God loved the world', so much and that 'all things were made through the Word'.

George had a studious frown, but the beginnings of a glint in his eye, as he considered what had been said.

"Combining them all into a single simple phrase then, 'God loved all things that were made through the Word'."

"That's a simple but very poignant way of putting it," remarked George.

Jay continued. "Distilling it down a little further, God poured His love through the Word to create the world!"

George's eyes popped open wide, his interest growing with every word Jay spoke.

"Distilling still further, God's love, poured through the Word, created the world."

A few seconds of quiet passed before George exclaimed, "That's very clever. Never thought of it like that!"

David's expression was one of bemusement. "What do you mean?"

"God poured His love through the Word, creating the world!" said George, exaggerating the words Word, Love and World.

David, however, mouthed the words, tossing them around in his mind.

George could not contain himself, exclaiming, "Well I'll be! It is simple, clever but so prophetic, so to the point. I wish college had used that in teaching, it makes so much more sense of the creation story. Never mind the 'big bang', 'creation', or 'evolution', it all started 'in the very beginning' with God's love being poured out through Jesus! Amazing! I'll drink to that one!" said George, raising his cup of tea.

They all laughed and the heavy air of earlier vanished as the morning mist on a summer's day.

With a childish expression on his face, George asked, "Do you have any more pearls like that?"

"Do you mean like the one the merchant sold everything for?" answered Jay.

After a small studious frown and thinking time, "Yes I do!" was George's answer as he roared with laughter.

"Can you remember what verse seventeen says George?"

After a little mumbling and thinking time, George responded.

"Not word for word, 'God sent His son to save the world, not to condemn it'. But wasn't that conditional, you have to believe in the Son?"

"Very good and yes. To believe in the Son was the final part of verse sixteen. Like many of John's words, they transcend both time, the spirit and natural realms. Although written much later, John looks back to the dawn of time, into the spirit realm, and sees the deep love Yahweh has for His creation. John also recognizes that humankind, because of your wilful nature, would be separated from God. But God gave up His Son to bridge and close that rift, not because humankind had done anything to merit the coming of the Son. In fact, just the opposite. But my Father loved the world so much that he sent me to be the bridge over and close that rift for any and all who seek to find it."

"But!" interrupted George, "That would mean God had sent Jesus long before many had repented, or even said sorry or I love you, to God!"

"Yes!" was Jay's simple reply.

"That's premature. God put all His eggs into one basket, so to speak. What would have happened if people had said 'no' or just ignored Jesus!" exclaimed George.

"That is what Yahweh's love does, he steps out first, to embrace, to love. Think of the Prodigal Son again. His father was looking for him and ran to meet him. The father ignored the son's words of repentance and humbleness, ordering serv-ants to fetch clothes, prepare a feast, but most of all to put a ring on his finger indicating that he was his son. Yahweh is exactly like that, as you cross the bridge, He runs to meet you, to celebrate and rejoice. Like the younger son, you too can say 'Abba' Father, I am sorry with all manner of protesta-tions. But, because you have returned and said sorry from deep within your heart, My Father is overjoyed, looking on you as seen through me! He will place a ring on your finger to show that you are His son or daughter. Paul tells you that you are adopted by my Father not just as children but as heirs of His kingdom, with all the rights that gives."

David asked Jay, "Can I cross that bridge even after what has been said about me?"

"Yes you can! You have already taken the first real steps, you both have."

George's cup clattered loudly as he almost dropped it on to the saucer.

"But I…" was all he could say before Jay continued.

"Theoretical knowledge is often man's knowledge, which hangs like the law and on defined rules: know this, learn that and so on. It also hangs on more subtle Pharisaical-style laws. You may be required to believe this statement and not that! Or, you acquiesce to my authority and interpretation of the scriptures regardless of the words of other teachers. But neither require a person to have an intimate relationship with My Father. That is secondary! The law-centred people are often challenged by the thought of an intimate relationship. To love and listen with an unrestricted open heart, to sit at my feet and listen much as Mary did, is a challenge too far for some. They find it difficult to let go of self, to be abandoned as King David was. All that comes as unrestricted love fills the heart, but it is not a requirement of knowledge.

"Father's only requirements are; you love Him from the deepest reaches of your heart and you look to Him for all things. Your reliance on theoretical knowledge, humankind's set ways and its laws block the love in your heart, George, just as much as David's adultery. Both of you have stepped on to the bridge, all has been forgiven, trust in My Father's love given freely through me. My Father sees you both, through me. My arms are open wide waiting for you to finally cross the bridge, to love Him from deep within your hearts."

Both men looked at each other with astonishment on their faces.

David looked at Jay long and hard. "You said earlier that you were Jesus. I have understood some of what you have said. How do I? What do I have to do?"

"Love Yahweh, My Father, with all your heart and love George and all your neighbours as much as you love yourself."

"It sounds too easy!" replied David.

"In words, it is easy. In practice, less so, because much of humankind does not want to understand or see the need of my Father's love. Many are still bound by the law and want visible, measurable penance in some form. Others will make it exceptionally difficult for both of you at times. But, and remember this; the strength of My Father is in me and I will help you overcome all obstacles," replied Jay.

"Oh!" exclaimed David.

A very deep silence covered the little group. George and David's faces moved from blank to concerned, from questioning to belief, from uncertainty to joy. Jay and Pete looked into each other's eyes, their smiles aglow with a sun-like radiance.

"George, you know how we used the words, 'Word' and 'world'."

George nodded in understanding.

"Often those who do not believe or who are wrapped firmly in the human interpretation and not the loving interpretation of the law will spread lies or distort the truth to confuse and harm those who are trying to cross the bridge. In essence, they try to change My Father's 'love in the world into a distorted love, which is filled with lies'. Not all are like this, but a number. Still others cause harm by their disinterest. If you take the 'distorted Love', the 'L' out of the 'world' you are left with the 'Word' once again.

Examine this distorted **love** with great care as it is very dangerous, is filled with **lies** and will ensnare and entrap the unprepared. Replace the 'O' in love with the 'i' from lies and it appears non-threatening as the word '**live**' appears. The distortion hides its real intent because it is reversed and actually reads '**evil**'. From the remaining letters appears the word **lose**! 'With and living under evil ultimately humankind will lose'." George sat for a few moments, mentally juggling the words and letters.

"Good grief!" said George. "So simple, yet again so profound. How deceptively easy to hide the real intent."

"Many lies distort My Father's love and Word in the hearts of many. It is not always possible to see or understand their real intent through the smooth words and apparently noble intentions. Those who are blinded by the 'i' of selfishness cause great hardship to those who are seeking My Father. Sadly, humankind sets great store by the five 'P's, Pride, Power, Position, Possessions, Popularity, all of which seek to distort and blind a person's perspective on life and a relationship with My Father. Love, Trust, Harmony and Perseverance are key tools that help those who are seeking My Father through the hard times. Listen to My Spirit as you read the word and fill your heart with an intimate desire for My Father. Look to me, believe in me, and His love will fill your hearts and His grace will provide..." said Jay, smiling broadly.

Chapter 16

The Journey Begins

Jay quietly looked at the three men as he wiped tears from his eyes and took a sip of tea. The silence was profound, secure, reassuring, like being under a warm duvet that enveloped them all. The other customers in the garden were oblivious to the table of four. No one noticed their interaction with each other, the tears, laughter, serious discussions, the holding and embracing of one another to reassure to show, 'I understand and I care.'

George looked at Jay with sorrowful, saucer-sized eyes. "All that you have said you meant from the heart didn't you?"

Jay smiled one of those warm infectious smiles that radiate out encouraging others to smile. "I did!"

"If we are so bad, why does God bother with us?"

"My Father loves His children; that is why! All have a seed of love, of true goodness in their hearts, that he alone can see. He tries to encourage that seed to grow, to respond to His love and to love Him in return. It is human pride that hides, enables and makes excuses for all the other 'sins' that causes human-kind to faultier and go its own way. My Father always tries to nurture, to help a child to grow, to love Him and for you to love those around you. If you truly love someone in your heart, you will go to any length to show them how much you love them. My Father is also like that and He wants you to mimic Him in your love for all humankind."

"How do I love those who have no time for me or want to stay within established boundaries or in the safe rut they have created?" said George with an exasperated tone.

Jay grinned and was about to speak, when Pete interrupted.

"Believe me, it is not easy. People will say you are wrong, a crackpot or even worse, but with perseverance, a smile, love, understanding, forgiveness and Father's Spirit guiding you, nothing is impossible."

"Oh!" said George, "But how do I get people to change and become God's children?"

"You don't!" was the firm reply from Jay.

"You point the way, you enable, you show My Father working in you. It is each individual person's own unique response to the love of my Father and My Spirit and their willingness to change that allows Him to change and guide their lives. Many hold on to the laws, to punishment and retribution. For many, on the surface they are simple to follow, black and white. If your indiscretions are not found out, no one cares. These misjudgements, millstones, hold them back, but they have until their last breath to say sorry and change. What they do not realize, accept, understand, or in some cases care about, is My Father sees and knows all that is in a person's heart. Looking into your heart, My Father can see every lie, every fault, that is hidden from others. But, when My Father looks into their heart, He can also see through the darkness to the spark of light within.

"If you think of the first four laws, George, they are positive commands, to do something! They are a hand, an arm gently guiding, showing the way. In gentler words, they are requests to love, to care. The love requested is not a shallow love, or a love at arm's length, or a love that gives only when it receives. It is a deep passionate, intimate love that has no boundaries.

It gives willingly before anything is reciprocated. A love that continues to give even if nothing is reciprocated. The final six are warnings against social actions that are dangerous and lead to a relationship and community breakdown. What they do not say is that, 'If you live in love and harmony we (six laws) become of no regard because love conquers all'. If you truly love, you will not harm a person. Just the opposite, you will help and protect them.

"My Father poured out His gift of love, freely without limits or restrictions, for you both through me, before you existed. I was given freely with only one condition – 'My Father's Hope'. Hope that the love offered would be accepted. Hope that, being accepted, it would be treasured. Hope that, in being treasured, it would flower. Hope that, in flowering, it would set seed. Hope that the seeds would be given away freely to others. Hope that those seeds given away to others would also germinate in their hearts.

"Think about my Father's 'gift of love' to each of you as the flower. Treasure it, encourage it to grow and give its seeds away to others.

"His 'grace', His 'gift of love', is poured out through me to both of you, to all of humankind. All you have to do is 'Embrace it!' George, you are one of many shepherd's to my Father's flock. Encourage them and share His love freely with all."

"So I can only guide and encourage those at church then?" queried George.

"Yes and no!" was Jay's emphatic response.

"Encourage and guide, be a shepherd from within the church flock, not leading it from in front or driving it from behind. You are equally fallible, so when you fall or make mistakes, accept help from others, be open. But most of all, be loving as

My Father is!"

"What about the 'no'?"

"The 'no' means not just the people within the church because all people are dear to My Father's heart. You need to reach out to all; firstly in love, then in deed, by example and then in and with the Word."

"But many are set in their ways and are happy with their relationship as it is."

"That, sadly, is true," said Jay, "But as an enabler, it is your responsibility to guide, to show them My Father working in you, to show them a different way, to encourage them to open their hearts. Many are divorced from My Father, as to some degree you are. However, you have started to change. Allow that change to continue, let it shine as a beacon to others. Use it as an illustration of My Father's love, in you, encouraging others who look at you and ask what is different, 'why are you as you are?'"

"What do I do when I get things wrong or say something that hurts another person?" questioned George.

Without hesitation, Jay responded, "You say you are sorry, one to one, from your heart and mean it. It is then up to the other person to forgive you from their heart."

"Oh!" was George's simple response.

"If your love for My Father is deeply embedded in your heart at the sound of His voice, at the touch of His spirit, your heart will glow and reflect His radiance into the world. People will see and be curious, others will see and question why you are so radiant today and still others, who have an understanding will ask, 'What has My Father's love shown you today?'"

"How can I? How do I fit in to all that you are saying? No matter what I do or say, no matter how I change, many will still ridicule or condemn!" said David with an anxious look and tone in his voice.

"What you have said, sadly is so very true," responded Jay.

"Firstly, let my Father's love and forgiveness into your heart. Let that love cleanse, strengthen, and help you on your chosen way. As that love flowers, reciprocate it, so you can be a living demonstration to many of the power of My Father's love. Like Zacchaeus and many others, My Father's touch through me changes the lives of many who have stumbled. Your words, your example, can be more powerful that George's. For those who have also stumbled to see you, a stumbled man, being restored, forgiven and enabled by My Father, it is the most powerful of witnesses."

"Oh!" was David's simple response.

Jay held a hand of both George and David, looking steadfastly in their faces, his eyes deep pools of love that flowed into theirs.

"George, you and David have long journeys to travel for which you are going to need the support of each other."

The two friends looked at each other questioningly. 'What journey? Why will I need support?'

"You have individual decisions to make which will negatively and positively affect others in equal measure. People will support you and understand while others will judge without real knowledge and condemn.

"George, open your heart fully, let the spirit of My Father fill your life; don't keep Him at arm's length or just for Sundays. Love, encourage and guide the flock from within that you are part of. Help them to draw near to My Father, by example, by your faults, by your willingness to forgive, but most of all by not being ashamed to show others your love of Him. The majority of the flock will follow, but for those that don't, seek them out and encourage them, help them to truly sense My

Father's love for them as an individual.

"David, can your relationship with Anne change into a loving and bright relationship as it once was? Take time to reflect before you decide, but having decided, be open, courageous, generous and loving towards both Anne and Simone.

"Don't press your thoughts, your expectations your moral standpoint on David, George, just be a good friend, a gentle listening ear. Most of all, do not desert him when people at work, in the community and the church, condemn. It is through those hard times that he will need a true friend.

"A similar request is placed on you David. George will need your support and friendship as he supports you. He will also need someone to share his pains, his hopes and, maybe if you can manage it, a time of prayer. Don't be concerned, it's nothing grand. Just a simple time talking together to My Father."

Both men looked at each other with great question mark expressions. Both looked at Jay and Pete, not knowing what to say.

George's hand tentatively took hold of David's. "I'll try to be with you whatever decision you make and will do my best to help and support you."

David's pallor had become the palest of grey. "Do you really mean that?"

"Yes I do!" was George's definite response.

"I'll try to be a good and supporting friend and, as Jay has suggested, maybe even pray with you, even though I don't go to church."

George responded with a radiant, "Thank you!" that was hotter than the sun.

The two looked deeply into each other's eyes, hands clasped firmly forming an invisible, unbreakable bond between them.

Sue approached the table. "Time gentlemen, we are closing now until six thirty, when you are welcome to return."

"Time?" queried David.

"But it feels like only a few minutes since we ate lunch. How can it be…?"

"Time is a human concept that has helped you fix one happening relative to another."

"Oh!"

Jay continued. "Time and space are without relevance to me as I can move from yesterday to tomorrow and from this place to another in an instant as I see them all as one, as a whole and not divided. Hearts have been opened, the five 'P's and their cohorts exposed and are being removed. In the freshly tilled soil of your heart; love, freedom, truth, understanding and many of their friends have been planted, watered and nurtured. Encourage the plants to grow, in yourself, in each other as you travel and in those you meet on your journey. Enable these good plants to grow, to flourish and to blossom. Continue to weed out the new shoots of the five 'P's' as humankind will shower you in their seeds. Do these things, not just in each other, but in all those you love, greet and work with. With My love, gentleness and understanding you can change the world around you."

"As you journey individually and together, in times of inner uncertainty, times of questioning from others, remember 'My Spirit is with you always'. This garden in the Black Swan will remain special to you both. Use it often for personal quiet and reflection. Bring others here too. Do not teach in the classical way, but show them me in you. I am in the sign of the Black Swan if you but open your hearts to see."

David and George frowned, mentally questioning Jay's words. Placing his cup down, David asked, "How are you in the pub sign?"

Jay smiled!

"Let me open your eyes to a world that reflects me in many hidden places. In history I too was considered a 'Black Swan', a 'Mucky Duck', by humankind and still am; scorned, my words considered a challenge to some, irrelevant to others, often dangerous to those in power. I was condemned as a blasphemer by those who were waiting for My Father's promise to be fulfilled. The waters I travelled were sometimes turbulent, other times placid, but always fruitful. The rushes in the pub sign are behind the Black Swan and signify and look like 'flames of fire', My Spirit. I have continued to send My Spirit 'in flames of fire' to encourage and help other generations to know My Father and me. I will do no less for you both! The seed pods are My Children filled with grace. They scatter the seeds of My Father's deep true love into the hearts of others. As you bring people here, encourage them by using the pub sign, make me accessible so that an intimate relationship may be formed. Use the 'Word' often but always keep in the front of your mind, 'Love My Father with all your heart and each other as you would want to be loved in return'."

George and David looked at Jay with wide eyes and said in unison.

"We will if you will help and guide us!"

Both laughed, realizing that they had said the words together – a new partnership formed?

With scones finished and tea drunk, the four headed towards the river pathway. Embracing each other in turn, they said their farewells. Jay and Pete turned and ambled towards the small plank bridge while George and David took the river path home past the mill race. Waving a distant farewell to their friends, George and David walked homewards with a new-found lightness in their steps. They laughed and discussed all that had gone on, without the bitter sweet roller coaster of emotions that had been a part of their journey to the Mucky Duck. They discussed the two new friends they had met, revelling in their insight and knowledge of their relationship and of their individual and personal situations. A new deep and profound love was developing inside each heart for this man Jay, his friend Pete and each other. For George and David, this new friendship was coalescing in their hearts and becoming a substance of great worth with each joyful step.

On the opposite bank, Jay and Pete watched with the radiant smiles of master craftsmen pleased with the work they had achieved. Both were bathed in a white, furnace-hot light that, second by second, increased in intensity absorbing their earthly forms till only a shadow remained. Jay expressed his inner thoughts as much to the birds and trees as to Pete.

"They both have uneasy journeys to make, but in time they will understand the meaning of the three gifts in their lives, given to me as a child all those years ago. With My Father's help, guidance and protection they will all become our brothers and sisters in My Father's family."

Epilogue

George and David are characteristic of many of us, as are their situations and responses to those situations.

George is in a position of authority and responsibility and has high ideals for himself and others. He is a man of letters who has lost his initial love and relies on knowledge alone. Full of good intentions, however, over time he is drawn into and schooled by a system that is ruled by the five 'P's. The 'lime light' and the flattery of others that tends to come with such positions has spawned the love of pride, power, position, prestige and popularity in him.

David, a more creative man, thrives on inspiration, ideas and the 'what if' and 'if only' from within and from the encouragement of others. His exciting work life is in stark contrast to a simple but torpid married life. With the introduction of Simone, another creative spirit, into his work life the contrast becomes more pronounced, with the almost inevitable results.

The laws we commonly use, handed down to humankind through Moses from God, ask us to love and be faithful firstly to God and then each other. Our two characters break the same law of adultery. George lacks a true love of God and is infatuated by the gifts the five 'P's offer him. David, however, breaks the more common interpretation of the same law with his extramarital relationship.

The Bible often speaks of God knowing and looking into the

heart of a person. God is able to look into and know the heart, seeing the intentions and hidden things of the heart that we are unable to see. We understand the heart as an organ that pumps blood and nothing more! That is its temporal practical role in the life of each of us. Yet humankind often refers to 'affairs of the heart' or 'the heart of the matter' or 'heart to heart' when we talk about our emotions, especially love and relationships. Dependent on how you, personally, read and interpret the Bible, God has loved humankind from the earliest of time. He has always wanted a special 'heart to heart' relationship with us and not a relationship based on what we 'do' for Him. For the believer, He has demonstrated His love for humankind in both spiritual and practical ways over the millennia.

Reflective thoughts and Images of the Five 'P's found in the Bible

PRIDE: Luke18: 9–14. The Pharisee in the Temple.

9 To some who were confident of their own righteousness and looked down on everybody else, Jesus told this parable: **10** "Two men went up to the temple to pray, one a Pharisee and the other a tax collector. **11** The Pharisee stood by himself and prayed about himself 'God, I thank you that I am not like other men – robbers, evildoers, adulterers – or even like this tax collector. **12** I fast twice a week and give a tenth of all I get.' **13** "But the tax collector stood at a distance. He would not even look up to heaven, but beat his breast and said, 'God, have mercy on me, a sinner.' **14** "I tell you that this man, rather than the other, went home justified before God. For everyone who exalts himself will be humbled, and he who humbles himself will be exalted."

Jesus begins his words on pride with: "To some who are confident of their own righteousness and looked down on everybody else." In biblical terms, righteousness is translated as being right with God. To be wholly and fully right with God (to His standard) is an impossibility. Is my heart pure, in tune with God every millisecond of the day and night? No, absolutely not and never will be!

God loves us, knowing that we are flawed and fallible and makes allowances for the things we do wrong. Pride is invasive and does and hides many negative things in a person's life. As in the case of the Pharisee, it fills the ego with much self-importance and blinds the 'eye of the heart' to many truths. Before God we are all equal, yet with pride in his heart the Pharisee did not say or indicate, or have any penitence, before God. And, in looking down with pride in his heart, he scorned the tax collector.

A representation of all the five 'P's are in this one passage.

a) He pridefully compares and judges the simple offerings of others while boasting about his own.
b) The Pharisee stands, presumably in a prominent position; the look-at-me syndrome.
c) He is a man of great wealth, great possessions, who fulfilled the letter of the law, or did he?
   Did he truly love God?
   Was he humble before God?
   Was he truly sorry for his mistakes accrued during the previous days?
d) The Pharisee was a man of power, of status.
   His words, his demeanour, exemplify this.
   His demeanour also suggests he was a man who was never wrong!

He was a man used to using and wielding power, possibly to his own advantage.

Saw himself as 'an equal to God', as a man who did not need to say 'sorry.'

e) In the eyes of many, he may have been a 'righteous' man following the requirements of the law, publicly 'but not in his heart'.

He may also have been popular, with some, because of the things he did and the great 'show' he put on.

POWER: John 8: 3–11. The woman caught in adultery.

3 The teachers of the law and the Pharisees brought in a woman caught in adultery. They made her stand before the group **4** and said to Jesus, "Teacher, this woman was caught in the act of adultery. **5** In the Law Moses commanded us to stone such women. Now what do you say?" **6** They were using this question as a trap, in order to have a basis for accusing him. But Jesus bent down and started to write on the ground with his finger. **7** When they kept on questioning him, he straightened up and said to them, "If any one of you is without sin, let him be the first to throw a stone at her." **8** Again he stooped down and wrote on the ground. **9** At this, those who heard began to go away one at a time, the older ones first, until only Jesus was left, with the woman still standing there. **10** Jesus straightened up and asked her, "Woman, where are they? Has no one condemned you?" **11** "No one, sir," she said. "Then neither do I condemn you," Jesus declared. "Go now and leave your life of sin."

The Pharisees and Teachers of the Law (All the Laws of Moses) had over time become hypocritical, not just in their keeping of the laws but how they were imposed on others. (The 'do what

I say, not what I do' syndrome). Jesus, throughout much of his ministry, challenged the Pharisees to fulfil the law themselves; to be truthful and honest and encourage others instead of making the law a burden on the people. The fourth commandment speaks of God's great love towards all those who 'Love Him and Keep His Commandments.' Jesus' challenge to those in authority was to fulfil the commandments themselves and love God from the heart. Many of the Pharisees depicted in the Gospels appear to keep God at arm's length, believing if they fulfilled the letter of the law, carrying out the practical aspects, nothing else mattered. To love God was an academic exercise or an issue to be debated rather than a 'living thing within their hearts'. Jesus pointed out many times and in different ways the hypocrisy (the dual standards) of the Pharisees, the majority of which were met with anger and hatred. How human even today! One exception was the clash concerning the woman caught in adultery. Misusing their authority, they tried to entrap Jesus and, if that failed, use Jesus' words to have the woman stoned to death! Jesus, in return, debated the issue by writing on the ground, challenging the life style and hearts of the Pharisees. The older Pharisees understood Jesus' written words (not known) and left without condemning the woman to be stoned to death. The older Pharisees understood the words and recognized that they were equally sinners, and therefore under the law did not have the right to stone the woman. These challenges of Jesus were, in time, met by the most ruthless of ways common to humankind throughout time, His death. Those in authority will often fight and misuse the power they have to maintain it, their position, privilege to protect themselves and further their own ends.

POSITION: Matthew 20: 20–28. A Mother's request.

20 Then the mother of Zebedee's sons came to Jesus with her sons and, kneeling down, asked a favour of him. **21** "What is it you want?" he asked. She said, "Grant that one of these two sons of mine may sit at your right and the other at your left in your kingdom." **22** "You don't know what you are asking," Jesus said to them. "Can you drink the cup I am going to drink?" "We can," they answered. **23** Jesus said to them, "You will indeed drink from my cup, but to sit at my right or left is not for me to grant. These places belong to those for whom they have been prepared by my Father." **24** When the ten heard about this, they were indignant with the two brothers. **25** Jesus called them together and said, "You know that the rulers of the Gentiles lord it over them, and their high officials exercise authority over them. **26** Not so with you. Instead, whoever wants to become great among you must be your servant, **27** and whoever wants to be first must be your slave – **28** just as the Son of Man did not come to be served, but to serve, and to give his life as a ransom for many."

The mother of James and John, possibly 'earthly' cousins of Jesus, asks Jesus if her two sons may sit at his right and left hands. As today, these special close positions to the central figure mark rank, favour and privilege gifted by the central figure. Like many a parent, she wanted the best of everything for her children and was willing to use family connections to try to achieve greater status for them. She was gently put in her place by Jesus saying to her 'that not only did those places come with a price, those who were to sit them were selected by God.' This mother's request caused jealousy and unrest amongst the other disciples. Jesus used his own life of service and not lordship as an example to them all.

POSSESSIONS: Luke 18: 18–27. The Rich Ruler.

18 A certain ruler asked him, "Good teacher, what must I do to inherit eternal life?" **19** "Why do you call me good?" Jesus answered. "No one is good – except God alone. **20** You know the commandments: 'Do not commit adultery, do not murder, do not steal, do not give false testimony, honour your father and mother.'" **21** "All these I have kept since I was a boy," he said. **22** When Jesus heard this, he said to him, "You still lack one thing. Sell everything you have and give to the poor, and you will have treasure in heaven. Then come, follow me." **23** When he heard this, he became very sad, because he was a man of great wealth. **24** Jesus looked at him and said, "How hard it is for the rich to enter the kingdom of God! **25** Indeed, it is easier for a camel to go through the eye of a needle than for a rich man to enter the kingdom of God." **26** Those who heard this asked, "Who then can be saved?" **27** Jesus replied, "What is impossible with men is possible with God."

The rich man tried to flatter Jesus, to no avail. When questioned by Jesus about keeping the Law, he said, "All these I have kept since I was a boy." But Jesus looked into his heart knew his love of wealth was greater and in v22 He asked the man to sell everything and give to the poor so he might have treasure in heaven. In the story of Job this situation is reversed. Job is 'tested' and literally loses everything, but not his trust in God. In the last chapter, Job 42: 12, it says, "That the Lord blessed Job's life more than the first." It then lists the great family and wealth Job was given by God. If, like Job, the rich man had put his reliance in God, the story's outcome could have been very different.

Sadly, the modern world, like the rich man, sets great store in what we have, the possessions we hold, their age, there brand name and so on. Negative advertising is subtle, using humiliation of self and others to promote and sell this year's must-have gadget instead of last year's. If we do not have the latest whatever we are branded poor or out of touch, dinosaurs. This continual provision 'of things' gratifies the here and now and, like a drug, needs to be fed anew as soon as a new model is manufactured. God's spiritual provision changes the heart, an anathema to many, but in doing so reduces the effect of the gadget drug! This spiritual provision feeds the inner person in a very different way and is renewed and strengthened, encouraging us for a lifetime.

POPULARITY: Luke 14: 12–14. At a meal with the Pharisee. **12** Then Jesus said to his host, "When you give a luncheon or dinner, do not invite your friends, your brothers or relatives, or your rich neighbours; if you do, they may invite you back and so you will be repaid. **13** But when you give a banquet, invite the poor, the crippled, the lame, the blind, **14** and you will be blessed. Although they cannot repay you, you will be repaid at the resurrection of the righteous."

Jesus is at a Sabbath (Sunday) meal with a prominent Pharisee. The guests are all 'well to do' men of the local area. Jesus asks why does he just invite all his friends and rich neighbours? It is a commonplace thing we all do. The merry-go-round of life requires I invite you this month, you invite me next month, and so on. The more invites, the more popular you are in the eyes of others and your own. Jesus suggests a philanthropic way to the Pharisee: the inviting of those in need and those who cannot invite you, so there is no tit-for-tat scenario.

Popularity, to be noticed, appreciated, is an emotion we all crave, like being the life and soul of the party. Sadly, there are those who selfishly 'hog' the limelight at the expense of others. If you are in the limelight, share it! Encourage someone less able to join you, but in a pleasant way, not by patronizing them or making sport of them. Help them to feel more important than yourself, to be wanted, needed, loved and appreciated by all around.

Two Foundation Stones

Dependent on your point of view The Bible is just a story or a book about our relationship with God. The Fall of Humankind, or the story described in the Bible, could be considered as the first foundation stone. Humankind is led astray by an entity with poor intensions. However, as the apple is eaten, knowledge is gained. How is that knowledge used? Firstly, the players hide, afraid, knowing that they have done wrong, doing the very thing they had been asked not to do! How childlike, how human. If you say to anyone "do not touch", "do not look", "do not sit" and so on the urge is to do the very opposite. In our story, God is walking in the garden and asks, "Why hide, what is wrong?" Adam explains a little, and then passes the blame for his actions on to Eve, who then passes the blame on to the entity!

What a picture of our modern day culture. Had an accident yesterday "that was not your fault", the blame passed on to someone else? The downside of knowledge is that it brings with it responsibility. If you know (have the knowledge) a fact to be true then to say otherwise is to lie or misrepresent the truth, or deliberately with intent mislead others. In our story, the entity misleads Adam with deliberate intent. Setting the story aside, the gaining of knowledge still has responsibility as an integral part. If a knowledgable person says, "Do not …

because it will harm …," should those in power or with responsible positions and ourselves not take note and act accordingly? Often the poorer attitudes of humankind take control. It is not financially expedient to … or politically it is not viable to … are some of the modern day phrases that are often used. These all stem from our poorer attitudes of, greed, power, position, popularity and so on. Knowledge, like the law, highlights our poorer attitudes, yet we accept their use daily. We make excuses and phrases that judge one to be acceptable, another not. Knowledge of what is acceptable and what is not is in us all, yet we wallow in the unacceptable attitudes quite happily, especially if we are not found out!

The second foundation stone, regardless of tradition or belief, is interwoven into the very fabric of our society: The Ten Commandments. The final six laws, 'the Social Laws', tell us how to behave and interact sociably with each other. However, like the Hebrew people before us, we have rewritten the ten laws and expanded them into great books. They are often quoted as if they were an unbending rod of steel with which we can control or subjugate our peers. That attitude, of righteous subjugation, is acceptable to most individuals until they are being 'beaten' by the steel rod in some way. The laws are written in the simple 'do not' form that humankind over the years has found hard to accept. We like the leeway to wallow in the mud; to steal and be given a 'sentence' befitting our rank or status, not the severity of the crime! Humankind is inclined to be judgemental, often harsh, when laws are broken and far less inclined to be understanding and forgiving. God, when asking Adam, "What was wrong," took time to ascertain the facts before acting.

Equally, humankind has the knowledge and ability to search through the facts before judging. However, many judge first, without the knowledge surrounding the circumstances of the crime. This may be a reflection of two things: their own hidden poorer attitudes. Secondly, the fact they are hypocritically pointing out the poorer attitudes of others while hiding their own, 'similar', poorer attitudes in their heart. It is the 'thank goodness I have not been found out, but, I am going to beat you because you have done wrong and have been found out' syndrome. Like a magician who distracts the eye, so the sleight of hand is not seen. If we truly face the mirror of truth, we all wallow in the mud of our distorted poor attitudes and it is those attitudes that colour how we interact, convict, malign, criminalize and judge others. What we would use as mitigating circumstances are not acceptable from another. Knowledge and responsibility, the 'first stone', should also have fairness and understanding to balance the scales of justice of the 'second stone'.

It's All in the Name

In our narrative, two different names are used when speaking about God. There are, dependent on tradition, some 140 names of God. Each name speaks of a different aspect of God's nature: God Almighty, In Heaven, Creator, of Justice, Forgiving, Our Father, My Beloved...

The name Yahweh (Yud-hey-vav-hey) is not used, but thought to be 'My Name' spoken of in Exodus 6: 2–3 when God was speaking in a more intimate way to Moses. Yahweh is the most holy and intimate of God's names, the very essence of who God is. To try and express all that this name implies is an impossibility. It would be like trying to describe the whole universe in detail with the knowledge we currently have, when we do not know anything about its furthest regions!

Father (Abba) takes the immensity of the unknowable and

condenses it into a very human figure and relationship form. Jesus used this term many times when seeking God's love, guidance, reassurance and in offering all things to Him. It is almost beyond comprehension that we can have such an intimate loving, caring, forgiving and personal relationship with the person who is God Almighty (El Shaddai). But we can!

The name My Beloved (Y'didi) was used by God at Jesus' baptism and on the mountain top. This truly reveals Yahweh's intimate love for His Son and that same relationship is there for each of His children.

The God of Love (El Ahavah) is waiting; to hear you call His name, to forgive our many mistakes, to encourage us in all things, to love us intimately as no other father can.

The GRACE of GOD

In the Compact Oxford English Dictionary the word grace has many uses. The fourth use reads: Grace – "(in Christian belief) the free and unearned favour of God."

In simple terms the love, the forgiveness, the understanding (and many other descriptive words) of God is available for us all. We cannot earn that favour (that love) by doing good works or some other similar action. The love is freely available it is there ready now for each of us. All we have to do is love God in return.

George's love towards God had grown shallow and cold as the five 'P's (his poor attitude) took control. No one else knew that George's relationship with God was on the rocks. George himself hid from the truth of his spiritual adultery, seeking comfort in tradition and doing 'good works' that pleased humankind.

David's love and knowledge of God was very superficial, stemming from his early school years. Yet he was conscious of his temporal adultery, not entirely from a faith standpoint but certainly from the anticipated judgement and condemnation of humankind.

Like our two friends, we are all sinners under the law one way or another. All of us without exception are 'Mucky Ducks'. The sins of some, like David, are in the public domain. The sins of George are in his heart and secret from the world. Both are seen by God, both should come under the jurisdiction of the law. The penalty under the law for all our sins, hidden and displayed would, like the woman caught in adultery, be death, but not necessarily by stoning. However, God through His sacrificial giving of His Son, paid the penalty for all our sins.

The love God has for all His children can be seen from the earliest of times. Unlike humankind, God sought the whole truth, the facts surrounding Adam's sin, before blame or an act of punishment was considered. The story of Adam, Eve, the serpent and the apple are well known. What is often missed by the listener in the reading is verse twenty-one.

Genesis 3: 21–24. Punishment tempered with Love.
21 The Lord God made garments of skin for Adam and his wife and clothed them. **22** And the Lord God said, "The man has now become like one of us, knowing good and evil. He must not be allowed to reach out his hand and take also from the tree of life and eat, and live forever." **23** So the Lord God banished him from the Garden of Eden to work the ground from which he had been taken. **24** After he drove the man out, he placed on the east side of the Garden of Eden cherubim and a flaming sword flashing back and forth to guard the way to the tree of life.

Before banishing man from the garden, because they were naked, God made clothes for Adam and Eve. Why? God didn't have to! He could have, but out of love He did not punish harshly! He banished, only to protect the 'Tree of Life'. Was He also saying, "I cannot trust you," so you can no longer stay in 'My Garden'? As part of their banishment from the garden, He could have sent them out in their nakedness and embarrassment. God Loved Adam and Eve as he loves each of us today and continued to provide for them as He does for all of us. Their flaw (their sin) was to listen to another who had ulterior motives. We all wallow in the mud of our poorer attitudes first seen in this story and discussed in the 'Two Stones'.

God's justice, however, was and is tempered with His Love. God's Love is freely given in practical, lifesaving, loving action reaching out to all. The 'black and white' grammar and intensions of the law, 'second stone' under grace, take on a kaleidoscope of colours. The ten laws become wrapped into one phrase that links God with humankind. 'Love God with your whole heart and all humankind equally'. God reaches out to us in love, all we have to do is love Him in return. In reading the Bible many, sadly, do not see His desire, His seeking of a loving relationship with His children. They only see God the warrior, dictator, who punishes unmercifully. However, if you look, read 'between the lines', of many of the stories, justice is balanced with love, anger with compassion, punishment mitigated with God's loving care. Under grace, the need for our punishment has been fulfilled once and for all, no buts, no what ifs, no quid pro quos. God expects nothing from us, only a love of Him that is deep from within our hearts. As our hearts open, God fills them with His love, removing guilt and shame imposed by humankind. He empowers, giving a knowing that reaches far beyond any knowledge, a supreme sense of being loved and many other gifts unique to each person.

George and David tasted that same forgiving love as they spent time in the bar, by the river and in the garden of the Black Swan. They had done nothing to merit God's love, but it reached out to their hearts and was offered regardless of their mistakes in life. All they had to do was accept (Jay) Jesus into their hearts to receive to receive God's bountiful gifts. We are all, in different ways, Georges and Davids with our own unique flaws. All we have to do is to truly open our hearts to a wonderful dynamic intimate relationship and receive God's boundless love.

All the NIV Bible quotations are from the Thompson Chain Reference Edition.